MELVIN INVENTS MUSIC

CLAIRE & MONTE MONTGOMERY

CBAY Books
Dallas, TX

Melvin Invents Music

Children's Brains are Yummy Books
Dallas, Texas
www.cbaybooks.com

Paperback ISBN: 978-1-933767-42-0
ebook ISBN: 978-1-933767-43-7
Kindle ISBN: 978-1-933767-55-0
PDF ISBN: 978-1-933767-56-7

Printed in the United States of America.

ONE

Fifty-two hundred years ago, along the shore of what's now known as the Gulf of Finland, but at the time was known as the Ozin, or "ocean," there was a tiny village called Grimstad, or "grim village."

Bear in mind that 3200 B.C. is a very long time ago—long before the formation of the countries that make up that part of the world today, or the things they're known for. Since there was no Norway, there was no Norwegian wood. Similarly there was no Danish Modern furniture, or for that matter, Danish Ancient furniture. And Swedish meatballs were simply called "meatballs."

The cities of Copenhagen, Oslo, Stockholm, and Helsinki didn't exist, and even if they had, they would have been hard to visit because bad weather and worse roads made it nearly impossible to get anywhere. As far as the people of tiny Grimstad knew, the entire world consisted of their town, their bay, and a few similar villages scattered up and down the coast of what is now called Scandinavia, but at the time was called Shivrkalt, or "Wow, is it cold here."

Most of the world had four seasons—spring, summer, fall and winter—but when you got far enough north, there were really only two: winter and getting-ready-for-winter.

And in Grimstad, getting-ready-for-winter meant fishing.

Nearly everyone in town was involved in the fish business in one way or another. There were the fishermen themselves, who during the precious four months of getting-ready-for-winter (let's just call it summer, to save time), set out in small sailboats and caught as many herring, perch, and salmon as they could bring back in their sturdy nets. There were the cooks, who did their best to bring variety to the town's year-round fish diet

2

by means of frying, grilling, or poaching. There were the farmers, who primarily grew side dishes such as barley, beets and potatoes—for man does not live by fish alone.

And there were the fishwives. These were not, as you might think, women who were married to fish (although the way their husbands smelled, they often felt like they were). These women *sold* fish at the open-air market in the middle of town by screaming at the top of their lungs about how fresh, tasty and affordable it was. This profession would later come to be known as "advertising."

Other important jobs in the fish-industrial complex included cutting it up; packaging it; preserving it by salting or smoking; building and repairing boats; making nets, hooks, and lines; and so on.

Another key fact about life in long-ago, far-away Grimstad had nothing to do with the way it felt, looked, or smelled but with the way it *sounded*. There was plenty of noise around (the fishwives, in particular, could really pin your ears back), but most of what people heard was random and disorganized, such as the scraping of fish scales, the sweeping of streets, the crunching of stale bread crusts, the snarling of dogs, or the cries of shoppers trampling one another to get to the best flounder.

And even the sounds that *weren't* random or disorganized went unappreciated, because no one had yet developed the skill of listening for order, meaning, or beauty. A woodpecker might be tapping out a fascinating rhythm on a hollow tree, or the night wind might whistle tunefully through the ancient evergreens, or a hot bronze ingot might ring out under a blacksmith's hammer, but these sounds would only register in the ears of a Grimstadian as, respectively, a bird, a breeze, and a bunch of banging.

As a result, something important, something beautiful, something spiritual, was missing from life in Grimstad.

In short, life was without music.

Think about what that meant!

To cite just one example: there was no

singing. You could talk, mutter, whisper, gossip, harangue, shout, babble, and filibuster till you were blue in the face, but you couldn't croon, warble, serenade, trill, or yodel.

You couldn't even hum.

When the fishermen put out to sea, they had no rousing sea shanties to raise their spirits. When a farmer cleaned out her chicken coops, there was here a chick, there a chick, but no E-I-E-I-O. And when an occasion called for the Shivrkaltian anthem—before a town meeting, say, or on National Halibut Day—people just put their hands over their hearts and mumbled the following:

> *Shivrkalt's our only home,*
> *Far from it we shall not roam.*
> *We pledge allegiance to its flag,*
> *And not to the flag of any other town,*
> *country, or district.*

Poetry hadn't gotten very far, either.

Curiously, the absence of music didn't stop

people from dancing. Scandinavians are known to this day for their passion for the waltz, rhumba, and foxtrot. But way back then, when Grimstadians got together for their regular Saturday-night socials, they just paired off and shuffled silently around the floor in a clockwise circle. This would go on for two or three minutes; then they'd stop, switch partners, and start shuffling again. If they really wanted to cut loose, sometimes they'd go in a *counter*clockwise circle.

So, that was life in Grimstad. You were born, grew up, ate fish, went to dances, got married, raised a family, did your job, hung out with your friends, grew old, and died—preferably during the summer, because the earth froze solid the rest of the time, which meant waiting until next June to get buried. People were reasonably content from day to day, but deep down—way deep down—every Grimstadian sensed that something was missing.

Especially Melvin.

When you think about it, the word "wait" really has two different meanings. There's the kind where you know how long you'll have to wait (until lunch, say, or until your next birthday), and there's the kind where you *don't* know (until a loose tooth falls out, for example, or until your big brother stops beating you up). The second kind of waiting, you'll agree, is generally harder than the first.

Similarly, there are two different meanings for the word "miss." You can miss something *known* (the skateboard you lost down a storm drain) or something *unknown* (a special, essential ingredient to life, whose qualities are a mystery but whose absence is driving you out of your skull). Again, the second kind is tougher to take.

Melvin *missed* music, but because there was no such thing yet, he was slowly being driven out of his skull.

TWO

Melvin was born on March 1, 3217 B.C., during a heat wave (ten below zero) to Lars, a fisherman, and Sonya, his wife. He was considered an oddball right from the start—a sound freak. Even as a baby, he was fascinated by noises of all kinds. Crickets interested him. Footsteps interested him. His mother's rocking chair *fascinated* him—rather than lulling young Melvin to sleep, the regular creak of the floorboards jazzed him up into a state of keen excitement.

When Melvin was old enough to feed himself, he would often bang a carrot against the table until he turned it into mush. Same with radishes. Anything that made an unusual noise when it was hit, scraped, dropped, rubbed, or blown into could captivate him for hours. Once Sonya made the mistake of bringing home some shells she'd found, and he spent a whole afternoon clinking them together and grinning. She finally had to put them back on the beach.

He learned how to speak right on schedule, just like any normal kid, but in between common sentences like "I'm bored" and "What's for dinner?" he would sometimes erupt in weird howls that were closer to the baying of wolves than to human speech.

It was positively creepy.

Of course Melvin's parents were deeply concerned about his odd behavior. Grimstad was a fishing town, and anybody who made as much noise as he did was likely to scare the perch right out of the bay. So Lars and Sonya decided not to have any more kids, just in case the next one came out even goofier.

"Maybe when he grows up and starts dating, he'll snap out of it," Sonya suggested to her husband one day while they were mending nets.

"Who's gonna date him?" Lars asked. "With

all the racket he makes, a girl would have to be crazy to go out with him. Crazy or deaf."

"He's handsome, though, you have to admit."

She had a point. By the time he was sixteen, Melvin had inherited his dad's broad shoulders and his mom's slender neck, and he moved with an easy grace that was quite attractive to girls— at least until they got close enough to hear him grunting and whistling and snapping his fingers. Then they crossed the street.

But there was one girl in town who didn't mind Melvin's "condition"—in fact, she found it kind of intriguing. Her name was Laila, and she and Melvin had been friends since they were tots. They were always going places and doing things together.

"Do you hear that?" Melvin asked Laila one summer afternoon while they were out in his dad's boat, checking lobster traps.

"Hear what?"

"The waves, those little waves hitting the side of the boat."

She cocked her head. "Sort of a slap, slap, slap?"

10

"Right. Only if you pay attention, it's not slap, slap, it's more of a slap, slap-a-dap, slap, slap-a-dap. Do you hear it?"

"I'm not sure."

"Listen harder. What else do you hear?"

She squeezed her eyes shut and concentrated. "I give up. What?"

"Niels the woodcutter is splitting logs on shore," he said. "Plus, the hull is squeaking every time we pitch forward and back. So it's really, like, chop, slap, squeak, chop, slap-a-dap, chop, slap, squeak." Saying the words made him smile. It felt like someone was tickling his brain.

"What makes you notice stuff like that?"

"I've always been this way. I hear patterns."

"How can you *hear* patterns?" She fingered the cloth in her woolen shirt, cloth that she'd woven herself. (Laila came from a long line of weavers, celebrated for their creation of the herringbone weave.) "I mean, you can *see* a pattern. But how can you hear one?"

"I don't know, I just do. And that's not all. I can make 'em up, too. Here, I'll show you."

11

In the bottom of the boat was an empty lobster trap, a semicylindrical wooden cage about two feet long with a gated opening at one end. Picking up a pair of marlinspikes—pointy pieces of metal the size of chopsticks, used for untangling knots—he bent over and started tapping on the trap. He matched each tap with the slapping and creaking and chopping from shore. The rhythm began simply, but he added layer upon layer of complexity, weaving it in and out of the other sounds like a bright piece of thread that runs through a multicolored tapestry. As he played, his face took on a faraway expression, like a person dreaming he can fly.

Watching him, Laila smiled, even though she didn't understand what he was up to. One of the most enjoyable things in life is seeing somebody do something really, really well.

Melvin built his solo to a stirring climax and finished up with three loud *thumps*, the last of which broke one of the trap's slender wooden ribs. Laila whooped with delight. "That was amazing," she said.

Soon they arrived in the shallow water where Lars fished for lobster. Each of the traps was connected to a float on the surface by a sturdy rope. Every three or four days, the ropes had to be hauled up, to see if any lobsters had taken the bait.

Melvin lowered the sail and dropped anchor. The first three traps came up empty, but the next line that Laila tugged on put up some resistance.

"Hey, I think I've got something," she said.

"Me, too," he answered. They began to pull in their lines hand-over-hand, but Melvin stopped her. "Hang on a sec." He leaned over the railing and plucked Laila's taut line like a bowstring, then his own. "Hear that?" he said.

"Hear what?"

"Yours makes a higher sound than mine."

"So what?"

"Why is that?"

"Mel, my arms are about to fall off. Can we discuss this later?"

"Sorry," he said.

They continued to haul in the lines. When

the traps broke the surface, Laila's was found to contain three of the big, spiny crustaceans, while Melvin's had only one.

"I just figured something out," he shouted, smacking his forehead. "The pitch that results from plucking a stretched cord is proportional to its tension."

She just stared at him.

"I've gotta get to the workshop," he said.

Lars was so happy when his son returned with the day's haul—fourteen lobsters—that he didn't make a fuss about the broken trap. Melvin volunteered to fix it and took it out to the tool-shed behind the house.

What Melvin had been trying to explain to Laila was simply this: if you stretch one piece of string tighter than another, the tighter one makes a higher sound. He proved this by hammering nails into the walls of the shed, stretching lengths of fishing line between them, and plucking them with his finger. Soon he had stretched strings all over the place, transforming the entire shed into a large, crude musical instrument.

There were problems with the musical shed, though: it wasn't very loud, it wasn't portable, and if you weren't careful, you could cut your head off walking through it. That's where the lobster trap came in. While he was drumming on it in the boat, Melvin had noticed that it made a satisfying, though small, noise. He concluded that the sound was leaking out between the ribs. But if a lobster trap could trap lobsters, maybe it could trap sound as well. He just had to plug the leaks.

Retrieving a sheet from his bed, Melvin wrapped it tightly around the trap, pounded a nail into each end, and stretched a piece of string between them. When he plucked the string with his thumb, it made a much better tone than his earlier experiments had. But now the sound was a little muffled, so he cut a round hole in the cloth, right below the string. He plucked the string again, and when a rich, clear note came pouring out of the hole, he went all goose-bumpy.

Melvin plucked and plucked his single note until

he got a blister on his thumb. Then, for variety, he stretched a second piece of string next to the first, followed by a third, fourth, fifth and sixth. As he had before, he varied the tension on the strings, giving each one a different pitch. He arranged the strings with the looser ones at one side and the tighter ones at the other. When he strummed all six strings, the device made a chord similar to the one that would—5,175 years later—open the Beatles song, "A Hard Day's Night."

Melvin had made the world's first guitar.

THREE

Well, that's not exactly true. The modern six-string guitar, which would eventually help make stars out of such artists as Chuck Berry, Eric Clapton, and B.B. King, didn't really make its appearance until about the fourteenth century. The rough contraption that Melvin fashioned was closer to what's now known as a lute. But he was definitely headed in the *direction* of a guitar.

Melvin spent every free minute of the next three days out in the shed, refining his invention. He quickly learned that there were other ways to get different pitches out of strings than by varying their tension. Long ones made lower notes than short ones, and thin ones made higher notes than thick ones. If he plucked them with a small, triangular piece of wood or seashell, the sound was louder still (plus, he didn't get blisters). If he pressed one of his fingers down on the string partway along its length, the vibrating part got shorter, so the note got higher.

All this experimenting required a lot of fishing line, as Melvin's father discovered one day when he couldn't find any. Lars's search led him to the toolshed, where he found his son sitting on the floor.

"Where's my fishing line?" he asked.

"It's all here, Dad, don't worry. I've just been experimenting." He picked up a loose lute string two feet long. "See? Good as new."

"Sure, if you want to fish in a puddle. Where's the rest?"

Melvin looked around the shed. The longest piece of string to be found was about six feet. "I guess I could tie some pieces together—"

"Is that one of my lobster traps?" Lars interrupted, pointing at the strange-looking device Melvin was cradling in his lap.

"Well, it used to be. Now it's a lute."

18

"A *what*?"

"That's what I call it, anyway. Here, I'll show you how it works." He bent over and plucked out a series of notes, some high, some low, some long, some short. They fit together into a happy, bouncy, lively pattern. "Cool, isn't it?" he said. "And the sound it makes . . . I thought I'd call that 'music.' What do you think, Dad?" But when he looked up, he found himself all alone.

FOUR

We haven't spoken yet about spiritual life in the thirty-first century B.C. The Grimstadians were a religious, if not quite devout, people. Every Sunday morning they would go to the church—a big, sturdy wooden building at the other end of Main Street from the town hall—and listen to a sermon by Grimstad's spiritual leader, the Hegoumen. He wore a long, dark robe and a red hat that was so tall, he had to crouch whenever he went through a doorway. His voice was deep and impressive, and he had a talent for stringing big words together, the better to call upon the gods.

The Shivrkaltians believed in dozens of gods— Drizl, God of Rain; Brine, Goddess of the Deep;

Vayzmir, Goddess of Indigestion; Ikeya, God of Affordable Furniture—and the Hegoumen was on a first-name basis with them all. Whenever you wanted more of something (like good luck) or less of something (like termites), you placed some coins in the Hegoumen's collection plate, and he'd put in a good word for you with the appropriate deity.

In addition to public speaking and acting as an emissary to the gods, the Hegoumen was the go-to guy if you had a business or family problem that wouldn't yield to ordinary methods. Melvin, who had ended up as the weirdest kid in town despite his parents' best efforts, fit neatly into this category.

"We have to take him to see the Hegoumen," Lars told Sonya one night as they were washing the dishes. Melvin was, as usual, out in the woodshed, tinkering with his new invention.

"Isn't that kind of drastic, honey?"

"Did you see what he did to my lobster trap? It's ruined."

"So what? You've got dozens. And you can

always buy some more fishing line. It's not like he's taking food out of our mouths."

"How do you think I catch fish, Sonya? Talk 'em into surrendering?"

"Okay, so he *is* taking food out of our mouths. You could stand to lose a few pounds, anyway."

"Hmph. Well, he obviously needs help, and we've tried everything else."

Melvin chose this moment to burst in with his lute. "Hey, check it out! I made my lute portable."

Sonya took a closer look. He had fashioned a strap and nailed it to the ends of the instrument, allowing him to sling it over his shoulder.

"Now I can play it and walk around at the same time. What do you think?"

Sonya squinted her eyes. "This cloth looks familiar," she said, fingering the strap.

"It should. I made it out of one of your bras." Melvin put on what he hoped was a winning smile. "You don't mind, do you, Mom? Mom?"

FIVE

The Hegoumen lived alone in the parsonage (a small cottage attached to the church) but did most of his work in his office, which was up in the church tower. At three stories high, the tower was the tallest structure in Grimstad. He liked it because he figured it put him closer to the gods.

At ten o'clock the next Wednesday morning, Melvin sat opposite the Hegoumen in the tiny office, his lute in his lap. The holy man stared at the ceiling, stroking his long, gray beard. Then he lowered his eyes to meet Melvin's.

"An evil wind blows," the Hegoumen began ominously. "Foul sounds beget fell deeds, and vice versa."

"Huh?"

"Your parents told me you've been acting up of late."

"I wouldn't call it 'acting up.' I'm trying some new things."

"Is that the erstwhile lobster trap, now in a state of disrepair owing to your willful and ruinous actions?"

"My dad says I ruined it. I say I improved it."

"Indeed. Show me of what you speak."

"No problem," Melvin said. In the past few days he'd made several modifications to his lute. He attached a long wooden neck to one end, and ran strings the length of the instrument. By pressing against the neck with the fingers of his left hand he could play individual notes one after another, or even several at once.

Now the Hegoumen listened carefully while Melvin plucked out a series of notes. The Hegoumen frowned. "Hmmmmmm," he said. "What do you call that? That row of sounds."

"A melody."

"And when you make several of them at once, what is that?"

"A chord."

"'Melody,' 'chord,'" the Hegoumen repeated, wrinkling his nose. "Where did you learn such words? Did a sinister spirit appear and hiss these blasphemous terms into your innocent and trusting ear?"

"Of course not. I made them up, because regular words didn't seem to fit what I was doing. I guess I hear things differently from other people."

"That's a bit of an understatement," said the Hegoumen. "Operate the device once more."

Melvin played the melody again.

The Hegoumen stroked his chin. "Are you possessed? Does an unseen hand move within you, bending you to its own nefarious purposes?" asked the Hegoumen.

"I don't think so. I'm just making music."

"Hmmm. 'Music,' you say. And just how long have you been afflicted by this disease?"

"It's not a disease, sir. Diseases make you feel bad. Music makes me feel good. It's like it's building up inside me, all the time, and when it comes out I feel—satisfied."

"Like burping?"

"Even better."

"Hmm."

"Here, you give it a try." Melvin handed over the lute, and the Hegoumen plucked out a few harsh, buzzing, random notes.

"I fail to see anything very satisfying about that," he said.

"I could give you a few lessons," Melvin offered.

"That's quite enough," the Hegoumen snapped, standing up so fast that his hat grazed the ceiling. He shoved the lute back in Melvin's hands. "Your condition presents a challenge, young man. I may have to consult several gods on this one. In the meantime, I suggest you convert this infernal mechanism back into something beneficial, and return to doing what your parents tell you to do. Even if, as you claim, you are not demonically possessed, life is too short to waste it making horrible noise that nobody likes."

Melvin wasn't about to take this sitting down, so he stood up, too.

"*I* like it, and my friend Laila likes it. And one

of these days, *everybody's* going to like it. Even the gods."

He turned and left the room, letting the door bang shut behind him.

SIX

The short summer raced by. The people of Grimstad busily prepared for the long winter—storing salt cod in warehouses, putting up jams and preserves in pantries, and so on. Homeowners sealed up drafty shutters and replaced loose roof shingles, anticipating the harsh winds and deep snows that lay ahead.

Melvin did his best to help his parents with their work, but music—which had become his single, overriding passion—kept getting in the way. When Lars lent him his hunting bow and sent him into the woods in search of wild game, Melvin returned empty-handed, having spent most of the day attaching a dry gourd to the bow to amplify the twanging sound it made when plucked. Dispatched to the market for a potato, he became entranced by the wailing voices of the fishwives and forgot what he'd come for.

Increasingly desperate to put his son on a useful career path, Lars sent him to apprentice under Ivar, the carpenter. For two weeks Ivar taught Melvin the basics of woodworking and cabinetry, then assigned him the simple task of building a footstool, giving Melvin the wood, tools, and plans. Melvin ignored the plans and made a new lute instead.

It was October now, and the first snow would fly any day. One chilly afternoon, Lars took his son out on the boat for a serious talk.

Melvin brought along his new instrument. It had a smooth, carved back and a piece of goatskin stretched across its belly, and its strings made a rich, resonant tone. He thought it might soothe his father if he strummed it while they talked. It didn't.

"Listen," Lars said testily as he steered, "we need to talk about your career."

"Shoot," said Melvin.

"The fishing thing doesn't seem to be working out."

"I know, Dad. I don't think I've got the knack for it."

"You didn't really click with hunting or carpentry, either."

"Right you are."

"You'll be a man soon. Have you given any thought to what you might do for a living?"

"Well, I'm glad you asked, because actually I *have*." Melvin took a deep breath. "I'm going to be a professional musician."

"A *what*?" said Lars, nearly letting go of the tiller.

"A player. An instrumentalist. A virtuoso. A troubadour. You know, like what I'm doing right now." He gave the lute a few more enthusiastic strums.

"You can't be serious! You expect people to *pay* you for doing that?"

"Well, someday, yeah . . ."

Lars couldn't believe what he was hearing. His son a musician, whatever that was. Throwing away a reliable career for a roll of the dice in show business! Lars had no way of knowing that parents would be having this exact same discussion with their teenaged sons and daughters for the next five thousand years.

"Not everybody needs to be a fisherman, Dad," Melvin continued. "There are farmers, weavers, builders—"

"Right. Because *those* jobs are important. In fact, they're essential to civilization. People need food and clothing and shelter."

"Well, they need music, too."

"How can that be? It didn't even *exist* until you thought it up a few months ago."

Melvin frowned. Lars was right—if you thought about it, music wasn't *really* essential. But it was essential to Melvin; he knew that now. Could he possibly be the only person on earth who felt that way?

"Listen," Lars said, forcing himself to stay calm. "I was hoping it wouldn't come to this, but I'm afraid it has. I talked with the Hegoumen yesterday. His brother, Gustav, runs a kind of a . . . home, for kids with . . . special needs."

31

Melvin was suddenly alert and defensive, like a cat that senses it's about to get a bath. "What kind of 'special needs?' " he asked.

"Well, according to the Hegoumen, a number of other children have been identified who suffer from some of the same . . . symptoms that you have. This Gustav fellow specializes in curing them at his . . . school."

Melvin stopped strumming when he heard the word "school." His own school years had been unpleasant—both of them.

"Your mom and I have been thinking," Lars went on, "that you might get along better under Gustav's care than here with us. He could help you to . . . fit in with society. You might even learn a trade."

Melvin tightened his grip on his lute. "I've *got* a trade. And what's more, I've got talent."

But Lars didn't get a chance to respond, because at that moment something jumped out of the ocean twenty yards away, arced gracefully, and fell back in the water with an enormous splash.

"Great leaping seafood!" Lars cried. "That's

the biggest fish I've ever seen!"

What Lars had seen was actually a dolphin, which is a mammal, not a fish, but he couldn't really be expected to know the difference—back then, people still had trouble telling cats and dogs apart.

"Take the tiller," Lars ordered.

Father and son pursued their quarry the better part of an hour, until they were within striking distance. At ten feet from nose to tail, the dolphin was too big to land with a net, so Lars brought out the harpoon and line that he kept for emergencies. He waited until the dolphin jumped again and flung the harpoon with all his might, snagging it in its dorsal fin.

The dolphin battled fiercely to free itself. Several times it swam beneath them, threatening to capsize the little boat. But Lars was an experienced fisherman, and by skillfully playing the monster of the deep, he eventually tired it out, reeled it in, and tied it to the gunwale.

Sailing home with their catch, Melvin couldn't help feeling sorry for the big gray beast. He understood all that circle-of-life stuff and knew it was a mistake to get emotionally involved with your dinner, but there was something about this creature that spoke to him. It looked intelligent. It even looked . . . well, sensitive.

Arriving back at the dock, Lars realized that he and his son couldn't possibly carry the prize home by themselves. Melvin stayed behind to keep an eye on the dolphin while Lars went in search of Borg, the fish butcher. On the way into town, Lars calculated that by preserving some of the meat and selling the rest, he'd be able to buy his wife that new wolverine coat she had her eye on.

As Melvin waited at the dock, he wrestled with several issues. The career discussion hadn't gone well, and he was questioning whether any- one else would ever see the value in music, and now here was this big gray thing staring at him with one of its big, black eyes, totally unaware that it was about to be carved up into steaks and served with a side of turnip greens.

The occasion seemed to call for music (to Melvin, nearly every occasion seemed to call for music), so he sat down and improvised a melody on his trusty lute. It was sad and sweet and fit his mood perfectly. Finishing the tune, he started over at the beginning . . . and to his astonishment, the dolphin threw its head back and joined in, chirping and squeaking along with the melody.

The dolphin could make music, too!

This was the deep connection that Melvin had been waiting for. For the first time, his creation had touched someone. Okay, it was a 900-pound dolphin and not something more practical such as, say, a disapproving parent or a cute girl, but you had to start somewhere.

Lars soon returned with Borg and several curious locals. Melvin ran up from the dock to join them.

"Wait till you hear what I just learned about the sea monster!" exclaimed Melvin.

Lars stopped in his tracks when *he* learned something about the "sea monster"—it was gone. Melvin was all set with an explanation—that it wouldn't be right to eat something you just performed a duet with—but when he saw the look on his dad's face, he decided it wasn't worth the effort.

SEVEN

In a few days it was all arranged: the Hegoumen's brother, Gustav, would take Melvin in for a year at his institution, the Shivrkalt Home for Hopelessly Eccentric Youth.

As the Hegoumen had explained to Lars and Sonya, Gustav's system for molding oddballs, square pegs, and misfits into productive members of society was based upon a highly scientific combination of encouragement, guidance, occupational therapy, and threats with a large oak club. Results were guaranteed. Melvin had resisted the plan as long as he could, maintaining that there was nothing wrong with him, but his parents stood firm. After arguing nonstop for a day and a half, all the fight had gone out of him. He was as pooped out as the dolphin.

"Maybe it's for the best," he sighed to Laila the evening before he left. "The Hegoumen says the first step in rehabilitation is admitting you have a problem. These people know what's best for me. And once I'm cured, I'll come back, and you and I can hang out. Everything'll be better than ever."

"But I like you the way you are."

"But I'll probably be a lot happier once I'm like everyone else."

"Look me in the eye and tell me you really believe that," she said.

"I am."

"You're looking at my chin."

So one bleak morning in late October, Melvin set off on snowshoes for the Home, a day and a half's journey from Grimstad. In his pocket were an apple, three sardines, and a letter from the Hegoumen. It read:

> *Dear Brother Gustav:*
> *This will introduce Melvin, a good-*

37

hearted fellow but somewhat head-strong and quite noisy. Although his parents are not wealthy, they can be trusted to pay for his room, board, and education either until he is cured or until they run out of money, whichever comes first.

Your admiring elder brother,
the Hegoumen

Melvin trudged across the white fields with a heavy heart. He missed Laila, who came closer than anyone else to understanding him; he missed his mom, who had cried so hard when they said goodbye that the tears froze on her cheeks; and he missed his lutes, one of which had been turned back into a lobster trap and the other burned in the hearth.

As he plodded along, Melvin didn't feel like humming or whistling. This was one of those rare times when he wasn't thinking about music at all.

EIGHT

The Shivrkalt Home for Hopelessly Eccentric Youth consisted of four long, low log buildings at the base of a mountain range. One building was the dormitory, where the Eccentric Youth slept (boys in one room, girls in the other). The second was Gustav's living quarters, the third was the cafeteria, and the fourth—and by far the largest—was the Occupational Therapy Center.

Coming upon the compound at dusk, Melvin didn't much like the look of it. There was a small jail in Grimstad, rarely used (usually it was too cold to go out and commit crimes), and this place reminded him of it.

Vaguely foodlike smells wafted out of the cafeteria, so he knocked on that door first. It was opened by a short, perky girl a year or two younger than he was.

"You must be Melvin," she said. "I'm Birgit. We heard about you. Come on in, they just served dinner. The food's pretty rotten here, but you get used to it. You want to meet the crew? Come on."

Inside the room were thirty or so kids, aged six to sixteen, sitting at long tables made from split logs. Birgit seized Melvin's elbow and dragged him over to one such table.

"Hey, everybody, this is Melvin. Let's give him a special S.H.H.E.Y. welcome, whaddaya say?"

The diners gave him the "special welcome"— evidently a cold, silent glare—then returned to their bowls of gruel.

Birgit turned to Melvin. "They'll warm up to you. It just might take a while. Here, have a seat. I'll do the intros."

Melvin reflected that this girl was in an amazingly good mood considering that she was, essentially, a prisoner in the middle of nowhere. He wondered whether her particular form of hopeless eccentricity was excessive chipperness.

40

"That's Pieter," she chirped, indicating a slender fellow with drowsy, half-closed eyes. "He's the coolest person here, but he talks funny. This is Rolf." Rolf, compact and muscular, continued to shovel down his dinner like a robot. "He likes to hit things. Usually not people, though."

Birgit pointed to an intense, serious-looking girl at the end of the table. She had finished her gruel and appeared to be writing something on a scrap of paper in her lap.

"And that's Dagmar. She has a crush on Pieter."

"Shut up, Birgit," the girl said without looking up.

Birgit didn't seem to mind this. "Dagmar has self-esteem issues. She's really pretty, but she's the only one who doesn't know it. That's why she hides behind that tragic pile of hair."

The last comment was right on target—Dagmar's hair was such an uncontrollable mop that Melvin couldn't tell *what* she looked like under there. Her bangs resembled a cornice of dirty snow building up on a roof. She shot Melvin a hostile look from beneath them, then went back to writing.

41

Birgit plopped herself down on the bench and patted the empty seat beside her. As it was the only vacant spot in the room—the other three tables were full—Melvin took it.

"Tell us about yourself, Melvin," Birgit continued. "What are you in for? Vandalism? Insubordination? Body odor?"

He reflexively sniffed his armpits. They seemed okay.

"Hey, I'm just jerking your chain," Birgit said. "Seriously, what landed you in this dump? Wait, lemme guess. You make too much noise, right?"

"Well . . . yeah, I suppose."

She gave him a knowing look. "Join the club."

A short, stout woman with iron-gray hair arrived at the table and placed a bowl of gruel before Melvin. It looked like the muck that collected in the bottom of his father's boat.

"I'm not really hungry," he said.

The woman grunted, pointed at the bowl, and folded her powerful forearms. She clearly wasn't going anywhere until he took a spoonful, so he did. The gunk was every bit as awful as it looked, but he forced down a mouthful. The gruel woman nodded and shuffled away.

"That's Olga," Birgit explained. "She does the cooking and cleaning. She's a mute."

"Seriously?"

"In all the time I've been here, I've never heard her speak a word."

"Wish I could say that about some other people," said Dagmar.

"Shut up, Dag."

The door at the far end of the room banged open and a large man in a heavy coat entered, pursued by a scattering of snowflakes. All the kids sprang to their feet and stood at attention. Melvin did the same, deducing that this must be the headmaster. In one hand he held his famous club; in the other, a small wooden object. He slowly raised it above his head. "Who . . . made . . . this . . . napkin holder?"

Gustav's voice wasn't much louder than a whisper, but it made Melvin shiver. Nobody answered, so Gustav repeated the question while gliding menacingly around the room, his piercing eyes probing each face for a telltale sign of guilt. It was no use trying to hold out; the headmaster could look right into your soul. At length a pale blond boy with a scrawny neck slowly raised his hand.

"Is something . . . wrong with it . . . sir?" the boy said.

" 'Is something . . . wrong with it?' " Gustav mocked. "It only holds five napkins! It's supposed to hold *six* napkins! How am I supposed to sell a six-napkin napkin holder that can only hold five napkins?"

"Use thinner napkins?" suggested Melvin.

Everyone gasped. Gustav turned and walked over to the speaker, the floor squeaking with every step.

"You must be Melvin."

"Yes, sir. Mister Gustav. Sir."

The headmaster scowled at him from beneath his bushy eyebrows. "My brother says you're a real troublemaker."

Melvin didn't really have any reason to defend the scrawny kid, whom he didn't even know, but he didn't like to see anybody get pushed around, especially over something as insignificant as nap-kin holder capacity.

"I'm not trying to make trouble, sir, I was just saying that with thinner napkins, maybe—"

"*SILENCE!*" roared Gustav. "Don't talk to me about napkin holders. I was manufacturing napkin holders before you were born! Why, I *in-vented* the napkin holder! Then I invented nap-kins, so people would have something to put in them! And I can say with considerable authority that this napkin holder here . . . is de-fec-tive!" He dropped the item on the floor and stomped it into kindling wood. Then he raised the club and slowly waved it back and forth below Melvin's nose.

"I've got my eye on you," Gustav said, spitting each word out like an ice cube. Then he spun on his heel and marched back out into the winter night.

The room was immediately buzzing with speculation. Some predicted that Melvin would be banished to the mountains to be devoured by timber wolves, others that Gustav would chop him into tiny pieces and make soup out of him.

Neither option sounded particularly appealing.

"Nice going," Dagmar said. "Now he'll just treat us even worse."

"I was only trying to help," Melvin said.

"Thanks. Don't do it again."

After dinner everyone went off to bed in the dormitory. The droopy-lidded Pieter showed the new guy around. Melvin quickly learned that the boy had a strange way of expressing himself, but by paying close attention, he could usually figure out what Pieter was getting at.

"Welcome to the crib, man. I bed down over here, and this is your flop. Fresh meat gets the spot by the door, so if Gustav comes bustin' in all up in a tizzy, you'll be the first one he unloads on. Kind of a blame-game thing. But there's no way around it, man. The way it is is the way it is, know what I'm sayin'?"

Melvin took this to mean that new arrivals had to bear the added indignity of being held responsible for anything that went wrong in the dorm.

Being closest to the door, Melvin's bed was

already the least desirable, but as a special wel-come the other boys had tied all his sheets in knots and doused them with water.

This is gonna be a long year, he thought.

Two hours later Melvin was still wide awake. He was scared, he was wet, and most maddening-ly of all, he had a new beat stuck in his head. The rhythm had begun as a simple drip-drip from an icicle outside the window, but by the time he had "Melvinized" it, it went, "Drip-drop droop-drop skadda-wadda bip-bop," etc. Without even being aware of it, he started tapping the beat out loud on his chest. He'd only played through it twice when, to his amazement, the exact same rhythm came back to him from the other end of the room, as if bouncing off a mountainside. Melvin played it again, and it echoed back to him again.

"Who was that?" No answer. "Rolf?"

"Cool it, cats," Pieter's voice hissed from somewhere in the darkness. "I'm trying to grab me some shuteye, man."

"Sorry, Pieter," said Melvin.

"Ain't no thing."

47

NINE

The next morning, after a breakfast identical to last night's dinner except that there was less of it, Melvin participated in his first Occupational Therapy Session. The Hegoumen had described this to Lars and Sonya as a creative, nurturing activity that developed young bodies and minds while teaching cooperation and citizenship skills. But as far as Melvin could tell, the only thing being developed was Gustav's bank balance, and the only skills being taught were hard labor and servitude.

It was, to put it bluntly, slavery.

The Occupational Therapy Center was a big, open workshop where three products were manufactured: napkin holders, doorstops, and lingonberry jam. Seven days a week, from morning to night, the residents of the Shivrkalt Home for Hopelessly Eccentric Youth toiled without cease, except for a five-minute break at noon and another at four, when everyone rotated jobs—the doorstop makers became jam makers, and so on.

Gustav was, above all else, a businessman. Once a month he would take a load of products up and down the coast on his sled, selling them at markets, trade shows, and door-to-door. He always got top dollar by claiming that the proceeds benefited troubled youth. But of course, he also charged top dollar to the *parents* of the troubled youth, for taking care of the poor little darlings.

He had his customers both coming and going.

Melvin spent his first shift whittling doorstops—simple, triangular wedges of wood. Thanks to his brief apprenticeship with Ivar the carpenter, this art took Melvin less than five minutes to master.

Napkin holders, made by nailing together three pieces of wood, were a little trickier. Melvin's benchmate, Rolf, demonstrated the technique.

"Left side, bottom, right side. And try to hit the nails square on. If you bend 'em, Gustav pulls your ears."

Melvin watched Rolf pound in a few nails with steady, even taps.

After a while, Rolf started varying his hammer blows—three fast ones followed by three slow ones, then a row of very fast ones, and so on. A thought occurred to Melvin.

"That *was* you last night, wasn't it?"

"I don't know what you're talking about," muttered Rolf, keeping his eyes on his work.

"In the dorm, after we went to bed. I made some noises, and then you made some noises."

"I didn't do anything. Ix-nay on the oises-nay."

Just then Gustav arrived to announce the shift rotation, and Melvin was sent to the Jam Room.

The Jam Room was actually a separate building—a brick shed just behind the Occupational Therapy Center where the sweet, red lingonberries that grew wild in the nearby forests were boiled with sugar in a pot that was five feet wide, five feet deep, and solid bronze.

Melvin's job was to keep a fire burning under the pot, which required him to go out and gather fallen branches. He was on his third trip to the woods when he heard something he'd never heard before—a single, clear, high note, like a bird's song, only long and sustained. It was coming from behind a thicket of trees. He made straight for the source of the sound, which turned out to be Pieter, sitting cross-legged in the snow, blowing across the end of a stick about eight inches long. He was only playing one note, but Melvin immediately recognized the sound for what it was.

Suddenly he understood.

"You've got it, too," said Melvin, stepping out from behind a tree.

"Got what?" Pieter replied.

"Music."

"Hey, I'm just, like, messin' around—"

"No, you're making music."

"Never heard of it."

"It's that thing in your head, in your ears. It's been with you since you were little. Everywhere you go. You can't get away from it. But you don't want to, anyway, right? Because it's really cool. Am I right?"

Pieter sat slack-jawed. This newcomer seemed to be reading his thoughts. "Man, you're blowing my mind," he said.

"That's why you're here," Melvin persisted. "You're *musical*. Like me. That's how you ended up in this place. That's how we all did!"

"That's not what Gustav says. He says we're here because we've got, like, demons in our heads, because we haven't worked hard enough, or something—"

"Hmm," Melvin said. "Can I see that?"

Pieter handed over the stick and Melvin sighted down it like a gun barrel. "It's hollow."

"Yeah, I dug out the middle with a knife."

Melvin blew in one end. Nothing happened.

"No, across the top, like this." Pieter took the stick and demonstrated, producing the same pure tone he had before.

"Wow. Can I borrow it? I promise I'll give it back."

"Yeah, I guess."

"Awesome," Melvin said.

TEN

The more Melvin observed the kids at the Shivrkalt Home for Hopelessly Eccentric Youth, the more certain he became that his theory was correct.

The muscular Rolf was always tapping his toes or drumming his fingers. Birgit liked to hit things, too, but she seemed to prefer objects that made a distinct pitch when struck, such as the hard wooden doorstops.

Dagmar was a hummer. You had to listen closely, but when there was a lull in the Arctic breezes that blew day and night, or a gap in motor-mouthed Birgit's running commentary, Dagmar could be heard going "mmmm-mmmm" in a high, pretty voice.

She started humming once when Melvin was seated next to her at dinner, but stopped the instant he joined in.

"Sure, mock me," she said.

"Huh?"

"I suppose you think that's really clever, making fun of people's handicaps. Hey, Birgit's kind of short. I bet you could come up with some really great zingers for her."

"I wasn't making fun of you, Dag. I was just saying *I* hum, too. It's fun!"

"I only let my friends call me Dag."

"And it's not a handicap, it's a gift. See, I have this theory that—"

"Pass the gruel, please," she answered curtly, withdrawing even deeper into her great mass of mousy brown hair.

Every kid that Melvin interviewed told a similar story. From infancy they had all "suffered" from the same "symptoms" that he did. They were "noisy and disruptive." They took an "unhealthy" interest in sounds. They weren't drawn to "normal" activities. When their parents became sufficiently concerned, they shipped the tykes off to the same "specialist," in hopes of a "cure."

But a musical person can't be cured of music, any more than a freckled face can be cured of freckles, or one and one can be cured of adding up to two.

Now Melvin had a choice: suffer through the next year in silence with all his creativity stuffed down inside him, and watch everyone else do the same—or blow things wide open.

The question warranted serious thought. After about five seconds of serious thought, he had his answer.

ELEVEN

Back in Grimstad, with winter well underway, the village settled into its rhythm of short days and long nights. Lars shoveled the walk and mended nets. Sonya cooked and cleaned. Things were certainly peaceful and quiet, but Melvin's parents had to admit that they missed life with their son, which, though often infuriating, had never been dull.

Across town, Laila was spending most of her time at the loom in her parents' living room. Now that Melvin was gone, she no longer felt inspired to weave colorful patterns. Day after day she produced gray, gray, and more gray. On occasion her spirits would lift briefly, and she'd add a touch of brown. She began to wonder if she'd ever see her best friend again.

Grimstad hunkered down like a sleeping polar bear and waited for spring, unaware that miles away, at the Shivrkalt Home for Hopelessly Eccentric Youth, a revolution was about to take place.

TWELVE

By now Melvin knew four things about music:

1. Some people had a talent for making it and others didn't;
2. Some of those who didn't possess the talent, such as Laila, liked it nonetheless;
3. It was somehow mixed up with emotions and could make you feel happy or sad or excited or reflective or nostalgic or anxious or relaxed; and
4. It was highly contagious, like yawning.

Now certain that he was onto something special, Melvin pursued the notion even further. What would happen if several people made music—playing different notes, or even different instruments—at the same time? Now, *that* would be something.

Melvin swung into action. Every night after the rest of the kids were asleep, he tiptoed out of the dorm, climbed through a window of the Occupational Therapy Center, lit a candle, and as quietly as he could, created musical instruments.

He started in the doorstop department. Doorstops normally came in three sizes (small, medium, and large), and by observing Birgit, Melvin knew that when tapped they made three sounds (high, medium, and low). Bo-ring. So Melvin whittled twenty-four, from an enormous one that could hold open the door of a castle all the way down to a tiny one just two inches long. He fastened them to a long, thin board in order of size, and by striking them with a pair of ballpeen hammers, found he could plunk out simple melodies. The instrument made a fun, spooky, rattling sound, like skeletons tap dancing.

Drums were next. From the Jam Room he took four empty wooden barrels of different sizes and stretched a piece of stout cloth across each end. Hitting them with sticks produced exciting, explosive sounds that made his pulse race.

From the forest he collected the straightest branches he could find, cut them into different lengths, and hollowed them out as Pieter had done. By fastening the sticks together side-by-side with long strips of birch bark, he created a sort of super-flute, with each tube sounding a different note. By skipping around from tube to tube, he could play any tune that came to mind.

Melvin stashed all of these instruments and waited for the right moment to make his move.

His big chance presented itself a week later when Gustav took a load of goods into town, leaving Olga to oversee the kids. As soon as the headmaster was out of sight, Melvin brought his row-of-doorstops-fastened-to-a-board instrument out of hiding, set it up smack in the middle of the workshop, and started improvising a melody on it with two small hammers.

"What's that thing?" asked Birgit.

Melvin answered with the first nonsense word

that popped into his head. "A xylophone."

"Does Gustav know you have it?"

"Nope," he said happily, offering her the hammers. "Want to give it a try?"

"I don't know if I should," she said. But there was something inviting about the contraption. She took one hammer and gave the instrument a few tentative *clinks*. When the earth didn't split open and swallow her up, Birgit took the second hammer and played several more notes. She liked what she heard. A lot. Inside of a minute, she was all over the thing, recreating the melody Melvin had invented and throwing in a few variations of her own.

"Keep that up," he said, and raced to the Jam Room, where Rolf was stirring the big bronze pot.

"Help me with these," Melvin said, digging the four drums out of their hiding place.

"What are they?"

"You'll find out."

They carried the drums into the main room, and Melvin arranged them next to Birgit. "Big drum, low noise, small drum, high noise, okay?

Just try to keep the beat." Rolf didn't have to be asked twice, and before long, Birgit's solo became a duet.

A crowd was forming. Pieter pushed through it. "Hey, man, isn't that my wooden thing, strapped together with a bunch more . . . wooden things?"

"Pan pipes," Melvin corrected, handing him the superflute he'd made out of Pieter's hollow stick and a dozen more like them. Pieter didn't take long to get the hang of the multi-note version, and his tuneful tooting turned the duo into a trio.

What was needed to really complete things, Melvin felt, was a lute. Trembling with excitement, he opened a drawer, dug through some wool blankets, and retrieved a beautiful wooden lute that he'd finished the night before. He plopped himself down in the middle of the action, brought out his pick, and started playing.

The music they made together was primitive and unshaped, but everyone could sense its potential. The quartet tossed their ever-changing creation back and forth like a beach ball; or maybe it was like a multicolored kite, swooping and diving on the changing winds that blew through Pieter's pipes; or a thundering waterfall, cascading over the solid rocks of powerful rhythm that pulsed out of Rolf's big drums.

The rest of the kids, swept up in the spirit, laid their work aside and gathered around the players. It wasn't so much a performance as a celebration. Melvin touched his cheek and was surprised to find it was wet with tears.

This must be strong stuff, he thought to himself.

So involving was this new shared experience that nobody noticed right away when Olga entered with her mop. When Birgit eventually spotted the intruder, she froze in fear. Even if the cleaning lady couldn't speak, she'd surely find a way to rat them out to Gustav—possibly with the aid of drawings. But Olga soon made it obvious that she was friend, not foe, when she gathered up the folds of her skirts, jumped up on a table and started dancing in her heavy wooden shoes, an expression of pure joy on her face.

You never know who's going to respond to

music, or how. Melvin wasn't sure whether minutes or hours had passed when Dagmar suddenly tapped him on the shoulder.

"I hate to break things up," she said, "but you might want to think about stopping pretty soon."

"Why?"

"I just looked out the window. Gustav's coming."

The announcement chopped the group off mid-note like an ax. Olga hopped down from the table and helped the players stash their gear in a big storage locker where she kept cleaning supplies. Everyone scurried back to his workstation, and by the time Gustav entered, the room had been restored to perfect order and his young minions were toiling in silence. But there was a subtle change. Gustav sniffed the air. Something had happened here, and whatever it was, he was definitely against it.

THIRTEEN

The near miss shocked the kids back to reality. Out of respect for Gustav's oak club, they let a week go by with no music-making of any kind. But they could only keep quiet so long—now that they'd had a taste, they wanted more.

One night at dinner, Dagmar, who usually kept to herself, plunked down next to Melvin and whispered in his ear.

"Meet me behind the dorm after dinner, and bring that funny-looking thing you made."

"My lute?"

"Yeah, that."

Melvin waited at the appointed meeting spot for fifteen minutes, listening to his teeth chatter. He was about to give up when Dagmar glided toward him out of the darkness, holding a folded piece of paper.

"Sorry I'm late. I was finishing up a poem," she said.

"Poetry! So that's what you're working on all the time."

A noise made them jump, but it was only snow falling from a branch.

"So listen, Melvin," Dagmar continued, "that was pretty cool what you did the other day. That whole music concept. But you need to give it some shape."

"What do you mean?"

"Like, structure, drama, unity. You can't just let it run on and on, like a river. It needs a beginning, a middle, and an end. Like a story, you know?"

Melvin scowled. Since music was *his* invention, he assumed nobody else had anything to say about it.

"What do you mean?" he repeated.

"I'll show you. That thing you guys were playing the other day. Play it again."

He swung his lute into position and launched into the tune with gusto.

"No, slower. Let it breathe a little."

"Like this?"

"Perfect. Now, just keep going, and listen." She unfolded the paper.

"Locked in the ice, how can I survive—"

Melvin stopped strumming. "Do you mind? I'm playing here."

"I know, you dope. I'm helping you."

"You're what?"

"Remember that day in the cafeteria, when I thought you were making fun of me because I was humming, only you really weren't?"

"Yeah . . ."

"Well, I thought I'd try humming and reciting a poem at the same time. Kind of a *sustaaaaaaa-ined taaaaaalking* thing. Get it?"

"Yeah, but while I'm playing?"

"Work with me here, Melvin. You provide the chords, I'll take care of the melody. And don't stop until it's over."

"How will I know it's over?"

"You just will."

He started again, strumming the strings softly. The chords supported the melody the way the foundation holds up a house. Dagmar sang over what he was playing:

> *"Locked in the ice, how can I survive,*
> *Not even half alive, unless there's some-*
> *thing out there,*
> *Alone so long, buried underground, but*
> *then I heard a sound,*
> *And it touched me in a way I've never*
> *been touched before."*

Melvin usually looked down at his hands when he played, but now he couldn't take his eyes off of Dagmar. Something about her voice seemed to go straight into his heart, completely bypassing his ears and brain. He was being touched in a way *he'd* never been touched before. She continued:

*"The thrill of a lifetime—it opened my
  eyes
It shattered my silence, and showed me
  the skies.
You taught me to stand, with one touch
  of your hand
The thrill of my lifetime—is you."*

When she came to the end of the last line, Melvin, without making any conscious decision to do so, stopped playing. The piece felt complete—adding anything else would spoil it, like a third eye or an eleventh toe. His mouth had suddenly gone dry.

"What do you call that—what you were doing just now?" he said.

"Singing."

"And the whole thing?"

"A song. Do you like it?"

"Very . . . very much."

"Knew you would," she said, tucking the paper in her pocket. "Listen, I need to get to the bunkhouse." She took a few steps, then turned back.

"By the way, you can call me Dag. If you want."
And she disappeared into the darkness.

Melvin stood rooted to the spot. Something weird was going on in his head and his heart and his stomach, all at the same time, as if he had just gulped down a cocktail of emotions that kept reacting with each other, like an earthquake in a chemistry lab, popping and fizzing and exploding like a fabulous, fiery, fireworks finale.

Melvin was in love.

FOURTEEN

A short time ago there had been no such thing as music in the world. Now there was not only music but instruments, melodies, harmonies, rhythm, songs, and a band to perform them. What would really come in handy now was a place to practice without getting busted.

This dilemma was neatly solved one day when Olga slipped Melvin a spare key to the Jam Room. Being made of solid brick (to reduce the risk of fire), the building's walls provided excellent soundproofing, allowing the players to make as much racket as they wanted.

Which is why, to this day, a bunch of musicians improvising together is called a "jam session."

Practice began every night at ten and ran for

about two hours. Melvin soon emerged as the natural leader. Although he recognized that the other four members played their own instruments (or in Dagmar's case, sang) much better than he did, he had a knack for putting everything together and keeping things moving along. He also functioned as a peacemaker, settling the internal disputes that inevitably arise whenever people try to create something together.

Dagmar, for example, complained a lot, mostly about Rolf. "Why does he have to play so loud?" she asked Melvin after the first rehearsal.

"He's a drummer. It's a loud instrument." It would be several thousand years before the singer-versus-drummer controversy was solved by the invention of the microphone, so all Melvin could do was ask Rolf to play more quietly while she was singing.

"How about when she's *not* singing?" asked Rolf.

"Go nuts," Melvin said.

Thus was the drum solo born.

Melvin wrote the band's first songs, with

Dagmar supplying the words, but it wasn't long before everybody started contributing. Pieter showed up at rehearsal one night with a new composition called "Daddy Cool." The entire lyric consisted of the phrase, "daddy cool daddy cool daddy cool"—words weren't exactly his strong suit—but the music was fascinating. It was much more difficult and intricate than anything the band had tried up to now, with a snaky melody twisting through a series of murky, sideways chord changes, all propelled by a driving, complex rhythm.

Much later this form of music would evolve into what's now known as "jazz," and the people who made or enjoyed it—male and female alike—would call each other "man," as a tribute to Pieter.

Rolf's compositions, as you might expect, favored heavy beats, and Birgit's were based on the bonelike *plink plank plunk* of the xylophone. Melvin was thrilled by the variety. The more styles the better, he figured.

The band practiced through the winter, and the more they practiced, the better they got. Melvin spent every spare moment making further improvements to instruments, such as rotating pegs that let him fine-tune his lute and a foot-operated lever that allowed Rolf to play the drums with his feet as well as his hands.

The other residents of the Home got involved in music, too. Groups sprang up like wild mushrooms, each with its own unique sound. Four of the better boy singers formed a quartet for singing harmony on street corners, only there were no streets, so they sang at the corners of buildings instead (being careful, of course, to post a lookout to let them know if Gustav was coming). Some of the older kids hummed soft melodies to the younger ones before bedtime, which had a way of making the little ones sleep better.

Muddy was a mournful fifteen-year-old named after his mood, which was always as low down and soggy as a mud puddle. Muddy's constant depression wasn't all that surprising, given his sad history—as a baby he'd been kidnapped from a sunny, peaceful coffee plantation thousands of miles to the south—but he discovered that he could cheer himself up by singing about how miserable he was.

A typical song of his was "Doorstop Blues," which went like this:

> *Well I woke up this morning—made a*
> *bunch of doorstops out of wood*
> *Said I woke up this morning—made a*
> *bunch of doorstops out of wood*
> *Don't know why they need all them*
> *doorstops.*
> *A big rock does the job just as good.*

There was no denying it: everyone was happier than he'd been before Melvin arrived at the Home. Work seemed easier, gruel tasted better, and even the grimmest, bleakest morning somehow seemed a little sunnier with a song in your heart.

But the most dramatic transformation was Dagmar's.

With every rehearsal, the once-shy, reclusive

girl became more confident, more self-assured, more alive. To top it off, she showed up at breakfast one morning with a snazzy, sassy, short haircut. The previous night, Birgit had waited till she fell asleep and whacked off the brown mop with a butcher knife. "Your look was hurting the band," she explained unapologetically.

"Who cares how we look?" asked the furious singer. "The important thing is how we sound. We're artists." She continued to fume and snort until Birgit showed Dagmar her reflection in a washbasin. "Wow," she said. "I have cheekbones."

Dagmar's improved appearance just made Melvin fall deeper in love with her, but he kept his feelings to himself. For one thing, he had no idea what to say to her. For another, she seemed a lot more interested in Pieter than she was in him. But sometimes when Dagmar sang, he found himself staring at her with so much desire and longing in his heart that he'd forget what notes to play, and everyone yelled at him.

Love was hard.

espite everyone's efforts to keep the band under wraps, it was only a matter of time before Gustav started noticing strange things. Napkin holder and doorstop production was down. Jam quality was slipping. Several times the headmaster awoke to faint, eerie sounds that seemed to be coming from the direction of the Jam Room, but whenever he went to investigate, the place was empty.

What Gustav found most troubling were the smiles he kept seeing on kids' faces. The little fiends were definitely happy about something, and he was determined to find out what it was.

FIFTEEN

If you own a musical instrument, you probably have a special relationship with it. It's not quite as much a member of your family as your sister, but you feel more connected to it than a tool or a bike, or even your cousin in Albuquerque.

Of all the newly minted musicians at the Home, Pieter had the tightest relationship with his instrument. He was always cleaning and polishing his panpipes, and often tucked them into his shirt during the day in case an opportunity to practice presented itself. At dinner Pieter made a habit of wolfing down his gruel as fast as possible so that he could sneak out into the woods for a quick tooting session. But one night when he stood up to go, Gustav put his hand on Pieter's chest and pushed him back onto the bench.

"Where are you going?"

"I'm finished, man."

The headmaster's eyes narrowed. "What's that in your shirt?"

"What's what?"

"There's something in your shirt."

"Yeah. Me."

"No, there are some kind of ridges in there. I felt them."

"Those are my ribs."

"Ribs run side-to-side. These are vertical."

"It's a family trait."

Gustav now cranked up his accusing glare to full power. "Stand up," he ordered.

Pieter did. The pipes fell out of his shirt and clattered to the ground. Gustav picked up the instrument.

"What is this?" he demanded.

"It's a napkin holder."

"Is that a fact?"

"Straight up."

"Where am I supposed to put the napkins?"

"You don't, like, really want me to answer that, do you?"

"Did you make this thing? I'll know if you're lying."

Pieter didn't have to lie. "No," he said.

"Then who did?"

No one answered. Gustav's blood pressure went up several notches. He began to pace between the tables. "I try to help you people," he intoned in a voice that mixed anger, self-pity, and doom. "And how do you repay me? With missed production quotas and lumpy jam. By making funny sounds in the middle of the night. And by going around smiling all the time."

Gustav zeroed in on Melvin like a vulture circling a field mouse. When he was directly opposite the suspect, he stopped pacing. "Now, I've got one question, and nobody goes anyplace until I get an answer: what's going on around here, and who's responsible?"

"That's two questions," Melvin said.

"Don't get cute with me, mister," Gustav hissed, thumping his club into the palm of his hand. "You know exactly what I'm talking about. Something's phony-baloney, and you're gonna tell me what it is."

"I refuse."

Gustav slowly raised his club above his head. "Do you still refuse?"

Melvin didn't move a muscle. His head told him it's a bad idea to risk getting thumped with a club for your principles—no matter how noble they are—but his heart told him otherwise. He suddenly felt very protective of music. It seemed worth cherishing, guarding, making sacrifices for.

"Categorically," he said.

Nobody budged. Nobody even breathed. Gustav raised his club higher. Birgit leaped to her feet.

"Don't kill him," she blubbered. "Yes, Melvin made all the instruments and taught us how to play them and hid them in the storage closet in the Occupational Therapy Center, but he didn't mean any harm by it."

"Aha!" cried Gustav. "I knew it!" He threw Pieter's panpipes on the ground and stormed out.

Birgit turned to Melvin. "I'm sorry, but I couldn't stand to see you get your brains knocked out."

"That was sweet, Birg," he said. "You didn't really need to mention the part about the storage closet, though."

"Oops," she said.

When the kids caught up with their furious headmaster in the Occupational Therapy Center, he was already heading for Olga's closet at top speed. But he found his way blocked—by Olga herself, her feet firmly planted, holding her mop like a special forces combat stick.

"I command you to hand over that mop," Gustav thundered, brandishing his club.

She tightened her grip. "The only way you'll get this mop is by prying it out of my cold, dead hands, you mean, rotten, underpaying, child-exploiting fink."

"You can *talk*," stammered the astonished headmaster. "Why didn't you ever say anything before?"

"My mother told me, 'If you can't say something nice, don't say anything.'"

"That was nice?"

"You should hear what I'm *thinking*," she snarled, and swung the mop, sending Gustav cartwheeling across the room.

"So you wanna play rough, eh?" he said, getting to his feet. A lump the size of a penguin's egg was forming on his head. "Okay. Bring it."

"I thought you'd never ask," Olga said.

Master and servant fought like tomcats, overturning chairs and smashing work tables into kindling. Olga wielded her mop with remarkable power, having developed tremendous upper body strength with twenty years of cooking, cleaning, and—above all—fluff-and-fold. Their cries of "oof," "*en garde*," and "take that" echoed from the rafters.

Gustav was taller, heavier, and approximately fifty times meaner, but Olga battled with the vengeance of a poorly treated employee with no pension plan. After faking Gustav out with a tricky behind-the-back twirling maneuver, she shattered his oak club into splinters with one explosive blow. Gustav sank to his knees, dazed and bleeding, his chest heaving.

"Olga. Have mercy. I'll do whatever you say," he pleaded, "just don't swing that mop again."

"Seriously?"

"Absolutely."

"Okay. I want you to get up, turn around, and walk out of here, and never come back."

Gustav scanned the room. Melvin and the rest of the kids were lined up behind her like a platoon of soldiers, armed with hammers, saws, and chisels. Recognizing that he wasn't exactly negotiating from a position of strength, Gustav scrambled to his feet, grabbed his coat from the hook by the door, and fled into the dark night.

The kids surrounded their liberator, cheering like mad.

"Olga," Melvin said, "you took a big risk for us. Why did you do it?"

"You made me dance," she answered simply.

fter some discussion, it was decided that Olga would stay on at the Home and look after the younger children until they were grown up enough to take care of themselves. The older ones would wait until morning and return to their hometowns. A few were nervous about doing this, as they felt they weren't completely "cured."

"Don't you get it?" asked Melvin. "There's nothing wrong with us. There never was. We're just a little ahead of our time. As soon as people understand what music is, they'll be glad to have us back."

"Yeah?" asked Dagmar. "Who's gonna make 'em understand what music is?"

There was silence for a moment. This was an excellent question, not just because of its practicality, but because it led Melvin to realize, for the first time, what his destiny was—to be not just a musician, but an *ambassador* of music.

"I will," he said.

"Correction," said Birgit, marching over to his side. The top of her head came up about to his armpit. "You *and your band* will. Right, you guys?"

Rolf, Pieter and Dagmar looked at the odd couple, then at each other. Sure, they had families back home. But this was something else entirely—a chance to make history.

Pieter spoke for all of them: "Dig it."

SIXTEEN

The next morning dawned clear and bright. Icicles dripped, streams gurgled, and green plants could be seen poking their heads through the melting snow.

Out in front of the dorm, Olga helped Melvin and the gang pack for their departure. "Be sure to come visit," she said, fighting back tears. "I'll keep some gruel on the stove for you."

"Thanks, Olga—thanks for everything," Melvin said as he fastened the instruments to Gustav's abandoned sled for the trip into his hometown of Grimstad, where he felt they had the best chance of launching music. People already knew him there.

On the way into town, the band discussed possible methods of introducing their new creation.

Birgit favored a gradual approach, with everyone splitting up and playing individually around town, but Pieter pointed out that this wouldn't take advantage of the groovy, swinging magic that happened whenever they all jammed together. "Let's just hop on a mellow riff and ride it on out," he said.

Melvin provided the winning solution. This being Saturday, the band would set up at the open-air market and give an informal, impromptu concert. "One song and we got 'em," he predicted confidently.

The first thing Melvin wanted to do when he got back to Grimstad was visit his parents, so he peeled off from the rest of the group, arranging to meet them later at the marketplace.

Sonya and Lars were happy to see their son after all these months, but they wondered why he'd returned earlier than they expected.

"Some of us sort of . . . graduated early," he explained.

"So you're cured?" asked Sonya eagerly. "You've

gotten all that"—she couldn't bring herself to use the *m*-word—"that *stuff* out of your system?"

"Well, not exactly. I wanted to talk to you about that. Some of the other . . . early graduates and I are going to put on kind of a . . . well, sort of an exhibition, down at the marketplace, of some of the things we learned, and it'd really mean a lot to me if you guys could . . ."

A familiar feeling settled in Lars's stomach like an undercooked crab cake. "It's not going to involve any of—the *stuff*, is it?" he asked, clutching his wife's hand.

Melvin tried to put on a smile, but it came out more like a grimace. "Well . . . not exactly . . . *that* stuff, but . . . well, actually, yeah. Music."

Sonya burst into tears. So did Lars.

"Where did we go wrong?" they wailed. Their son left them there, sobbing into one another's arms.

SEVENTEEN

The market was a beehive of activity when Melvin caught up with his companions and started setting up equipment. He was still upset by the encounter with his folks, but his gloom evaporated quickly. It was a beautiful day, and the shoppers were glad to be out in the sun after the long winter. The ice that had covered the bay for eight months was breaking up, and the fish-wives were heralding the arrival of the season's first fresh pike and smelt.

"What do you want to open with?" Rolf asked.

They knew nine songs by now: "Thrill of a Lifetime," "Local Talent," "Great Day in the Morning," "Rock Solid," "Hornet's Nest," "Heat of the Moment," "One Big Happy Family," "Daddy

Cool," and "Doorstop Blues," which Muddy had given the band as a goodbye present before splitting for warmer climes.

"Let's do 'Thrill,'" Melvin suggested. "It's a good attention-getter." He glanced over at Dagmar to see if she would acknowledge that he'd chosen her "special" song, but she was busy doing something with her hair.

Pieter raised his instrument to his lips. "Swing easy, man. Just wail," he said.

"Want me to count it off?" said Rolf.

"Count it off, baby," said Melvin.

"One, two, three, *huh . . .*"

They tore into the song's introduction. Being only five people, and without microphones, speakers, or amplification of any kind, the band wasn't much louder than a modern-day string quartet, but what they lacked in volume they more than made up for in enthusiasm.

Heads turned at the very first note. A few curious onlookers wandered over, then several more. Melvin was scanning their faces to get a sense of how the act was going over when he recognized a familiar one. Laila was coming toward him through the gathering crowd.

"Melvin? Melvin! It *is* you!"

"Laila! Hey, I'm so glad to see you!"

"Why aren't you at that school? Who are these people? And what's all this stuff?"

"It's a long story. I'll tell you later—"

Just then Dagmar stepped out in front of the band to claim her solo spot. Her transformation from bushy-headed introvert to charismatic performer was nothing short of startling. The tight sealskin miniskirt and scarlet lips may have had something to do with it, but the real shift was one of attitude. The word "diva" popped into Melvin's head. He turned back to Laila, who was wearing a brown smock.

"Listen, I'm kind of in the middle of a tune here."

"What's a 'tune?' "

But Dagmar was in place and ready to sing the first line.

"Locked in the ice, how can I survive—"

Now the buyers and sellers were *really* paying attention. Their weekly routine at the marketplace had gone uninterrupted for years—until today. And they weren't happy about it.

"It's Melvin, Lars's son!" exclaimed one concerned shopper standing near the band. "He must have escaped from the Home."

"And he's brought some of his fellow inmates with him," added her scandalized friend. "What are those evil machines they're operating?"

Melvin overheard this.

"They're not evil, they're just instruments," he tried to explain.

"What did he say?" asked Helmut, the haberdasher.

"I think he said they're instruments of torture," explained Borg, the butcher.

The seed of mass hysteria began to take root.

"These kids are sick," exclaimed a cautious young mother. "They've come to spread their disease!" She produced a handkerchief and covered her daughter's mouth.

Melvin kept strumming away with a big smile

pasted on his face.

Inge, loudest of the fishwives, approached the band, followed by two of her co-workers. "What's all this racket about, then?" she cried. "I'm trying to close a deal on some haddock!"

Dagmar looked to Melvin for guidance. She'd never been heckled before. He gave her an encouraging look, and she continued bravely.

> *"I knew it would take a lot to thaw my heart,*
> *To bring me out—"*

"I'll thaw ya out, dearie," Inge cackled, seizing a bucket from a nearby vendor. Then she raised it with her spindly arms and dumped its contents—a gallon of brine-soaked sardines—right over Dagmar's head.

The young starlet gasped, sputtered, and wiped her eyes. Though she had no mirror, Dagmar correctly guessed that the sardines had done extensive damage to her hairdo. She stomped off, leaving salty footprints.

"That'll teach you to interrupt a place of business, ya hooligans," Inge said.

"Yeah, why don't you take your racket somewhere else," hollered her companion. Others pitched in, and soon nearly everyone was jeering and booing the intruders.

Still playing, the rest of the band looked to each other in sheer panic. Pieter, desperate to keep things rolling, launched into a wailing solo but halted abruptly when someone hit him in the head with a well-aimed octopus, setting off a free-for-all.

An open-air fish market provides an angry mob with a great deal of ammunition. Beneath a steady hail of clamshells, tuna tails and vegetables, Melvin and his would-be troubadours gathered up their instruments and what was left of their pride and beat a hasty retreat.

" 'One song and we've got 'em,' " Rolf gasped as they ran, shielding themselves from the barrage with their instruments. "Right."

"Shut up and run," Birgit said.

Laila's parents were still at the market selling cloth, so she brought Melvin and his bedraggled band back to her place to get cleaned up.

"That is so cool, what you guys can do," she said, wiping octopus juice out of Pieter's ear.

"Not exactly the majority opinion, man," he mumbled.

"All right, so I made a mistake," Melvin said. "Maybe we opened with the wrong song."

"We did *not*," Dagmar pitched in as she shampooed brine out of her hair. "Rolf was playing too loud. He scared everybody. And Birgit was out of tune."

"A xylophone doesn't *go* out of tune, Dagbreath," Birgit shot back. "It's a fixed-pitch instrument."

"Well, *somebody* was out of tune," Dagmar muttered, "and it sure wasn't me."

Melvin sensed that she was looking at him. He checked. She was.

He sank into a chair with his chin in his hands. How could this be happening? A few days ago, they'd all been a team, a family. How could a single bad experience smash everything to pieces? And the crack about playing out of tune, what was *that* about? He'd have to have a word with Dagmar, bandleader to singer.

Melvin stole another look at her, to see if he was still in love. He was. His resolve melted like an icicle in the sun.

"Okay, Dag, I suppose I should've re-tuned before we started. But Pieter has a point. We didn't handle this right. *I* didn't handle it right."

"We just need to find another way to show these people what we can do," the always-sunny Birgit said. "They'll love us; I know they will!"

"You know what, though?" said Laila. "For a minute there, you almost had them. People were starting to enjoy themselves."

"Yeah? Was that before or after that guy nailed me with a trout?" Rolf grumbled.

"No, really," Laila continued. "They were getting into it. *I* was into it, I couldn't stop bobbing my head, tapping my feet . . . in fact, it kind of made me feel like—I don't know, maybe . . . like dancing."

"I'm happy for you, Laila," Dagmar said, "but can you stick with the program here? We're talking about our music, not your feet."

"No, wait a minute," Birgit said. "Olga told us the same thing, last night. She said we made her dance!"

"That's right!" said Melvin. "Hey, maybe there's some kind of connection between the music and a desire to move the body about rhythmically."

"Excuse me, didn't I just say that?" asked Laila.

EIGHTEEN

Grimstad's town hall was just as drab as everything else in the village: a big, square building with brown wooden walls, untouched by color or ornament. Since tonight would be the first dance of spring, though, someone had spruced things up by attaching bouquets of daffodils to the window shutters and hanging a wreath of wildflowers above the door.

That afternoon Lars had told Sonya he was too upset by their encounter with Melvin to attend the function, but she insisted. It might take his mind off the family crisis, if only for a few hours.

The evening began as it always did, with dancers pairing off and shuffling in a circle. There was some talk of the afternoon's events, and people congratulated one another for defending the marketplace against the invaders. Someone told a joke that cracked everybody up, and Helmut, the haberdasher, loosened his tie.

It was time for Melvin to put his plan into action.

Strictly speaking it was Laila's plan, as she was the one to point out the connection between the new thing called "music" and the old thing called "dancing." She and Melvin had been outside a window since the sun went down, waiting for just the right moment.

When the next dance began, Melvin signaled to Rolf, who had arrived early and set up his drums in a coat closet inside the town hall and was now peering out through a crack in the door. Rolf started thumping out a rhythm on his big bass drum, quietly at first but with increasing volume.

Unaware that they were doing it, the dancers on the floor gradually fell into step with Rolf's steady beat, and when he added a series of accents on a smaller, second drum, some found themselves complementing their steps with a lilting shuffle.

"It's working," Melvin whispered to Laila. "Give Birgit the signal."

Laila slipped around the corner to another window, where Birgit was waiting with her xylophone. At Laila's sign, she added a peppy counterpoint to Rolf's drumbeat. A few of the dancers looked around to see where the sound was coming from, but Birgit was so short that her head didn't even rise above the sill. Besides, they were too busy swirling around the floor to the bubbling, pulsing beat that flowed around and through them.

Now Melvin began to strum his lute. His chords wafted into the hall like the scent of spring itself. Pieter was stationed on the roof. As soon as he heard Melvin join in, he did, too. His swinging flute-tooting filtered down through the shingles and onto the crowded dance floor.

In the middle of the throng, Lars held Sonya close in his arms.

"You're dancing awfully well this evening,

darling," she said. "You haven't kicked me in the shins once."

"Is that a fact, my little guppy? You seem especially light on your feet yourself."

Lars glanced around the room. Something was definitely up. Couples were spinning and whirling everywhere, inventing intricate new steps, gliding to and fro as if on skates. "You don't suppose it has something to do with those sounds from outside, do you?" he asked as he dipped his wife dramatically.

"Outside? I thought they were inside my head."

Now Laila's parents came tangoing through, low to the ground. Sonya was astounded. The weavers, notorious for being the worst dancers in Grimstad, usually spent the evening lurking in the corner, making rude comments about everyone else's outfits. But here they were, kicking up their heels with gusto.

"Pick it up, you two," Laila's father urged. "You're behind the beat."

"What's that mean?" asked Lars.

"I have no idea," Laila's mother answered, and

the two of them tangoed off with a peal of giddy laughter. Outside the window, Melvin and Laila were beaming at each other so hard that their faces hurt. Now it was time for the final test—bringing the band inside.

As Rolf kept pounding on his drums, Melvin and Laila went around the corner to where Birgit was concealed. They picked up her xylophone and carried it right through the front door as she continued to play. They put the instrument down next to the coat closet and threw open the door to reveal Rolf, hammering at full volume. Melvin added his lute to the mix, and a moment later, Pieter burst through the front doors, blazing away on his pipes. Now the band was in tight formation and full swing, and nobody had lifted a finger to stop them—that is, until Inge and three of her fellow fishwives arrived.

"It's them!" Inge hollered in a voice that would scrape the barnacles off a boat hull. "The hooligans from the marketplace! Get 'em!" All four blasted their way toward the band, scattering couples like bowling pins. But now a curious thing happened. Every step the fishwives took brought them deeper under the rhythm's spell. Halfway across the dance floor they fell into step with each other, and by the time they reached the band, they were snapping their fingers. Someone hooked Inge's elbow and spun her around, hoedown style, and soon all four would-be attackers were swept into the swirling throng.

When the song ended, there was a breathless moment of silence. Then somebody spontaneously started beating the palms of his hands together. The rest of the dancers followed. The noise was like waves crashing.

"Run for it!" yelled Pieter, startled. "They're gonna start throwing stuff again."

"No they're not," Birgit corrected, noting the expressions on their faces. "They like us. They really like us!"

The quintet raced through the rest of their numbers to a packed dance floor. When Melvin announced that they were out of material, the crowd demanded that they simply play the same songs over again—which they did. Three more times, in fact.

A little after midnight, the dancers and play-ers ran out of gas, so the evening was declared over. Birgit hugged Pieter. Rolf hugged Dagmar. Laila would have hugged Melvin, but she couldn't get close to him because the townspeople were mobbing him and peppering him with questions. Would he like to audition their daughter? Where was the group playing next? Would they consider performing at a wedding or bar mitzvah?

Melvin's parents found themselves at the cen-ter of a lot of attention, as well. But what Lars and Sonya wanted most was to talk to their son.

"Honey," Sonya said, "can you ever forgive us?"

"If you'll forgive me for ruining your bra."

"It's a deal."

Lars threw his arms around both of them in a big, fishy hug. Melvin didn't mind the smell one bit.

In a secluded corner of the room, unseen by the others, the Hegoumen observed the aftermath of the most successful dance in Shivrkalt's history.

Something significant had occurred. The citizens of Grimstad had seemed somehow transformed, empowered, liberated, by what they'd experienced. Nothing like that had ever happened in church— even after his best sermons. He furrowed his brow and stroked his whiskers nervously.

NINETEEN

The Hegoumen's fears were well-founded, as he learned when he entered the church the following morning . . . and found it completely empty. The entire town was still sound asleep. Dancing and carrying on until after midnight can really take its toll, and sometimes a solid ten-hour snooze is the only cure.

"I've lost them all," the Hegoumen moaned, wringing his beard like a dishrag. "Those children are more powerful than I. Perhaps they are themselves deities of some sort—the Gods of Strange Noises or something."

The members of Melvin's band woke around noon, in comfortable beds with clean sheets. The village had not only taken the group into their hearts but into their homes as well. Norbert the baker and his wife were putting up Dagmar and Birgit in their spare bedroom, and Rolf and Pieter were bunking with Ivar, the carpenter. This was *way* better than life with Gustav.

Melvin moved back in with his folks. The family dynamic was turned upside down now that their son was a hero. They let him sleep late on Sunday, tiptoeing around the kitchen to keep from waking the young genius. When Sonya heard Melvin stirring, she brought him a breakfast tray with juice, fresh rolls, and a kippered herring.

"Thanks, Mom. You're the greatest," he said.

"It's the least I can do," she answered, then backed out of the room and softly closed the door.

TWENTY

Spring was off to a great start, at least as far as Melvin was concerned. Practically overnight, he had gone from zero to hero. He was doing work he liked. He and Laila were able to pal around together whenever he wasn't rehearsing with the band out at Ivar's place and she wasn't helping her parents make cloth. Mostly they talked about music.

"Explain it to me again," she said one day as they were walking along the beach.

"I'll try. Okay, listen hard. Do you hear that?"

She listened hard. "Hear what?"

"Well, there's our footsteps, okay? And the waves are coming in, about every six steps, so it's, like, step step step step step step *swoosh*, step step

109

step step step step *swoosh*. You know. Patterns."

"I guess I'll never understand it."

Melvin frowned. Creating music was a lot easier than trying to define it. He made another attempt. "When you play a song you wrote, it's like crossing a river on stepping stones, blindfolded, only you don't need to look where you're going, because you're the one who put the stones there in the first place. Now do you get it?"

"Not quite. But it must feel great to master something like that."

"Master it? I don't think you can ever master it."

"Why not?"

"Because the better you get at music, the more there is to get better *at*. So in a way, the more you know, the less you know."

"That sounds frustrating."

"Frustrating? Are you kidding? It's the best feeling in the world—"

The smile vanished from his face. Laila looked ahead to see what had derailed him. Fifty yards up the beach, two people were sitting in the sand, talking and laughing.

"Hey," Laila said. "Isn't that Dagmar and Pieter?"

"Let's go back," Melvin said.

"What's the matter? I was just starting to understand what music is."

"I'm not in the mood to talk anymore."

"What are you in the mood to do?"

"Practice," Melvin said.

People started drifting back into church on Sunday mornings, but things had changed. The congregation would arrive late and leave early, and the Hegoumen had to work twice as hard to hold their attention. He was definitely losing his power over them. In an effort at damage control, he delivered fiery sermons on the evils of music, warning that these strange new sounds "were certain to anger the gods, resulting in righteous retribution, catastrophic cataclysm, and disastrous doom."

Right in the middle of one such lecture, he heard somebody whispering in the front pew. "Pardon me," he said, "but is there something you'd like to share with the rest of us?"

"Oh, sorry, Your Holiness," replied the whisperer. "I was just telling my wife how much I enjoyed dancing the mambo with her last night, and how much I was looking forward to doing it again next Saturday."

"Isn't that special," said the Hegoumen through clenched teeth.

TWENTY-ONE

Spring blossomed into summer, and music blossomed right along with it. It seemed to be everywhere. Basic musicality is far from uncommon, and soon Grimstad was positively crawling with singers and players.

People started making their own instruments. The first ones were based on Melvin's early designs, but they quickly branched out into many forms. The lute would eventually give birth to the dulcimer, the koto, the bouzouki and the balalaika. Pieter's pipes would one day evolve into the clarinet, the saxophone, and—to the everlasting annoyance of jazz purists everywhere—both the bagpipes and the accordion.

On balmy spring nights, young men took to

113

serenading their girlfriends from beneath their windows. In order to take full advantage of these private concerts, some of the girls had small platforms with railings installed outside their second-story bedrooms. This was the origin of the balcony.

Melvin was commissioned to write a melody to go with the Shivrkaltian anthem, and he came up with a doozy. With Dagmar's help he also reworked the lyrics a bit, so that it now went:

> *Dear Shivrkalt, our only home,*
> *Far from you we shall not roam.*
> *We sing your praises day and night,*
> *By evening star and morning light.*
> *Your mountains old, your flowers new,*
> *Your forests green and ocean blue,*
> *Remind us that we must be true*
> *Dear Shivrkalt, dear land, to you.*

Everyone agreed that it was a big improvement over the old one. Digby the blacksmith—who was as surprised as anybody to discover that he possessed a terrific baritone voice—organized a town choir to sing it.

Champion fishwife Inge, now an ardent supporter of the new art form, found an ingenious way to put it to use. She had a knack for coming up with simple, catchy melodies, and whenever she belted one out across the market in her ear-splitting soprano, customers couldn't help but notice. Here's a typical example:

> *Codfish, beautiful codfish!*
> *Still so fresh, it's flopping around.*
> *You should try it, boil or fry it.*
> *It's only half a kroner a pound!*

Thus was the jingle born.

But music had its drawbacks as well, the most insidious being the tendency of some songs to get maddeningly stuck in your head. Pieter's jazz ditty, "Daddy Cool," proved to be one of these, causing people to wander around with their fingers in their ears, muttering nonsense syllables in an attempt to dislodge it. But the only way to get one tune out of your head was to replace it with another, so Melvin was in constant demand as a songwriter.

Because of the way he felt about Dagmar, a lot of his songs were about love and romance, with an emphasis on heartbreak, longing, and woe. He tried to keep his emotions under control, but he still turned into a quivering bowl of lingonberry jam whenever Dagmar sang. As a result she had him wrapped around her little finger.

"Birgit keeps trying to upstage me, and Rolf is rushing again," she complained to him one day after practice.

"I'll talk to them about it."

"Also, I need a new outfit."

"I'll see what I can do."

"Plus, I need to skip a couple of rehearsals. I'm doing a press interview day after tomorrow."

"Why does that mean skipping *two* rehearsals?"

"I can't give an interview without a manicure, silly." She showed him the back of her lovely, graceful hands.

Melvin felt his knees go weak. "Hey, uh, I saw

you and Pieter on the beach the other day."

"And . . .?"

"Well, you know. I was just curious what you guys were talking about."

She gave him a look that was half pity and half disgust.

"Band stuff. Sheesh." And she walked away.

Melvin was miserable. Dagmar had a crush on Pieter, and Melvin had a crush on Dagmar, and Laila had a crush on Melvin.

"If only everybody could just shift over one crush," he thought.

TWENTY-TWO

You might be curious by now about what happened to Gustav after he was driven away from the Shivrkalt Home for Hopelessly Eccentric Youth. He had spent the night in a hollow tree, with only the clothes on his back and a burning desire for revenge in his heart to keep him warm. In the morning, he struck out for points unknown, in search of new victims to exploit.

Gustav wandered aimlessly, stopping in towns where he could pick up odd jobs—cheating a widow out of her life savings here, taking candy from a baby there—but all the while he was keeping his eye out for that "one big score" that would re-establish him as one of the Bronze

Age's pre-eminent con men.

As spring and summer wore on, he began to hear rumors of a new phenomenon: a band of youngsters based in tiny Grimstad, who had audiences lined up around the block to experience something called "music." The smell of someone else's success worked on Gustav the way blood in the water works on a shark, and as fast as his creaky legs would carry him, he headed for the house of his brother, the Hegoumen.

Grimstad's onetime spiritual leader was sitting in the parsonage, cooking up schemes to get back in charge of his flock, when a rap at the door roused him. He opened it and was astounded to find his younger brother standing on the porch.

"Gustav," he cried. "What a pleasant surprise! Tell me, what vicissitudes of fate have delivered you to my doorstep? To which unexpected development do I owe the unanticipated pleasure of your visit? How did you—"

"If you give your jaw a rest, I'll tell you," Gustav snapped, barging in and helping himself to the

Hegoumen's favorite chair.

The brothers spent the next hour filling each other in on recent developments. They discovered that most of the developments were rotten, and furthermore, that the same headstrong, ill-behaved, vexatious teenager seemed to be the source of all their bad luck.

"My congregation is getting more out of Saturday evening than they are out of Sunday morning," moaned the Hegoumen. "They drum their fingers and tap their feet while I'm talking. Sometimes they even hum."

"You? What about *me*? I had a booming business, and the next thing I know, I'm freezing my butt off in a tree trunk."

"If only there were some way to get rid of him," said the Hegoumen, twisting his beard into a knot.

Gustav didn't have a beard, so he just twisted his chin. "Maybe there is."

His brother's expression brightened. "Rope? Dagger? Poison? I think I have a hatchet somewhere—"

"No, you holy terror. I have a plan that'll solve *both* of our problems."

"It's a pretty good hatchet."

"Just leave everything to me, okay, Heg?"

TWENTY-THREE

When Melvin learned that Gustav was in town and staying at the parsonage, his first impulse was to throw a large stink bomb through the window, but the urge passed. His band was riding high—two sold-out shows every Saturday night— and by charging half a kroner a head and sharing the proceeds with the band, he was earning money for the first time in his life. It felt great. Why should he let the presence of a corrupt old headmaster—*former* headmaster at that—bother him?

A few days later Melvin was surprised to receive a message from Gustav, inviting him over for lunch. He said he wanted to make amends and had something important to discuss.

"What can it hurt?" thought Melvin. "He

doesn't have any power over me now."

When Gustav opened the door of the parson-age wearing a pair of his brother's pink bunny slippers, he looked a lot less threatening than he had as a club-wielding dictator.

"Great to see you, Melvin," he said. "I'm just finishing something up that I believe you'll find quite interesting. Make yourself at home. My brother's out of town at a Hegoumen conference."

Gustav cordially ushered Melvin into the din-ing room, where a large canvas stood on an ea-sel. "Of course, this is just a sketch. What do you think?"

On the easel was a full-color drawing of Melvin's band up on stage, playing to a packed house. Melvin and his lute were prominent-ly featured out front. It was a good likeness, he thought, although he appeared somewhat tall-er than in real life. A strange word was painted across the top in bold block letters.

"Who are the Mel-Tones?"

"The name of your band. Kind of a combina-tion of 'Melvin' and 'Tones.' Clever, huh?"

"I never thought about giving us a *name* . . ."

"Well, you can't expect people to keep calling you 'Those Five Kids Who Make All the Noise.'"

"I don't understand. What's this about?"

Gustav struck a confident pose and went into the sales spiel that he'd been practicing for days. "Melvin, I'm a simple businessman, nothing more. When I see someone with talent, ability, my natural instinct is to ask myself, 'What can I do to help this person achieve his potential?'"

"Is that what you were doing with us back at the Home?" asked Melvin testily. "Helping us 'achieve our potential?'"

"Tut tut," Gustav said. "Why dig up the past? Besides, I'm well beyond petty schemes now. I'm talking about big ideas. Huge ones. Like this." He gestured to the poster again. Melvin bent over to examine it.

"What's this mean, 'Coming to Your Town?'"

"It's a tour. The Mel-Tones are going on a trip."

"A trip?" said Melvin suspiciously. "Why? It's not like people don't dig us here." (He was beginning to pick up some of Pieter's lingo.)

124

"You're not seeing the big picture," Gustav said. "You guys may be huge here in Grimstad, but believe me, you ain't seen nothing yet. I'm gonna make you even *huger*. That's why we're going on the road. We'll hit every city, town, and village. Even the hamlets. I'm telling you, Mel, these yokels won't know what hit 'em. You'll be the biggest thing since fire."

Gustav walked across the room and opened a closet. "Hey, check this out." He brought out a short black jacket and held it up so that Melvin could see the back. Like the picture, it was emblazoned with big letters that read, "Melvin and the Mel-Tones—Grand Tour."

"Wow," Melvin said.

"One hundred percent reindeer hide. Supple, waterproof, and it wipes clean with a damp cloth. A customer of mine over in Frikburg makes 'em." Gustav helped Melvin slip the jacket on. It fit perfectly.

"Well . . . I'd have to check with the rest of the guys about the tour, to see if they're up for it."

"Oh, you don't have to worry about that."

"I don't?"

"Not a bit. And do you know why? Because you're the *leader*. Those kids'll follow you to the end of the earth."

Melvin fingered the genuine walrus-tusk buttons on his new jacket. "Plus, I don't know how my folks are gonna feel about all this."

"You kidding? With all the dough you'll rake in, you can buy your old man a new boat. A fleet. Heck, an armada."

"Really? An armada?"

"Besides, it's not like you're traipsing off into the wilds by yourself. I'll be along as kind of a . . . chaperone, a manager. Looking out for you and the rest of the gang. And all I ask in return is a small portion of the proceeds, just to cover my expenses. I'd say nine out of every ten kroners we take in should do it."

"Nine out of ten? Isn't that a lot?"

"Mel. What I'm offering you here is something money can't buy. I'm offering you celebrity."

Actually, Melvin was right about the money. Nowadays that ratio is reversed; managers typically take ten percent, artists ninety. But he'd stopped listening anyway. A big ball of happiness was growing inside him. Soon it would be big enough to include the whole world.

"So whaddaya say?" said Gustav, extending his hand. "We got a deal?"

Melvin took it. "We got a deal."

Walking home from the parsonage, it occurred to him that Gustav had never offered him lunch.

TWENTY-FOUR

The other band members reacted to the news of the tour in different ways. Pieter and Rolf put up the most resistance.

"*Gustav*?" said the incredulous drummer. "The same guy who had us in prison? Who made us work like slaves, and paid us off in cold gruel?"

"I'm telling you, everything's different now. He wants to *help* us. He knows all about business and promotion and a bunch of other stuff. It'll be a lot of work, but he thinks we can be really successful. Not just in this hick town, but all over!"

"I dunno, man," Pieter said. "Something about this whole scene doesn't click. Doesn't groove."

"Are you nuts? It'll be awesome!" said Birgit. "We'll go new places and meet new people, and everywhere we go, we'll spread joy and happiness and goodwill. And we'll stay up all night, and it'll be like a great big party, only it'll never stop!"

Dagmar was on the fence. "I'm not saying I'll go," she said as she curled her eyelashes. "But if I do go, I'll need my own dressing room. That's non-negotiable."

"That's the first thing I said to Gustav," Melvin lied. "I insisted on it." He figured he could always try to arrange something later.

"Really? With fresh flowers and bottled water? And honey for my throat?"

"I'll milk the bees myself."

"Melvin, you are totally the coolest," Dagmar cried, throwing her arms around him and giving him a big kiss.

"I don't think you milk bees," Rolf muttered.

"When do we leave?" asked Birgit. But Melvin didn't answer. He was still reeling from the kiss, ears ringing, head spinning, heart thumping. Being the leader definitely had its advantages.

The Mel-Tones embarked on their Grand Tour a week later. It had been a week crammed with preparation and rehearsal. Laila worked harder than anybody, making brightly colored cloth and sewing it together into eye-catching stage outfits for the whole band.

Laila had planned to go along on the tour, to take care of all the tailoring and cleaning and such, but at the last minute, her parents got a big order for sailcloth, and she had to stay home to help out.

"I'll be thinking about you every day," she told Melvin as she handed him his knapsack. He didn't answer, as he was distracted by the sight of Dagmar up ahead, sharing a private moment with Pieter. They'd been sharing a lot of private moments lately.

"How about you?" Laila persisted. "Will you be thinking about me, too?"

"Oh, sure! You know I will."

"And we'll write each other, okay?"

"Definitely."

"And as soon as I get caught up, I'll come out and visit."

"Uh, right. That'll be great . . ."

"You like the suit, don't you?"

"It rocks. Look, Laila, I've gotta go help Rolf strap his drums onto his donkey. See ya, okay?"

"Sure," she said, brushing a tear from her eye before he spotted it. She didn't want Melvin to worry about her feelings, on top of all the other stuff a bandleader has to think about when he's preparing to leave on a Grand Tour.

"No, Rolf, put the bass drum on his butt," Melvin hollered, and rushed off. Laila smiled after him. She was so proud.

TWENTY-FIVE

The first stop was in Grind, a small salt-mining town. Gustav had traveled there a few days earlier to talk up the show. He was a born salesman (he once sold six doorstops to a family who lived in a one-room cave) and by the time the Mel-Tones arrived, he'd whipped the locals into a frenzy of anticipation. This wasn't as difficult as you might think, since the people of Grind were grateful for anything that broke up their routine. If you think fishing is dull, you should try salt mining.

It was a beautiful summer evening, so the Mel-Tones performed outside under the stars, lit by tiki torches. The band had learned a bit about showmanship by now. Instead of freaking everybody out with a flag-waving opener, they started small—just

Dagmar, accompanied by Melvin's lute—and built from there. By the time all the players were onstage and rocking, the crowd was partying like—well, like salt miners.

The concert was a smash. Three encores. Afterward, Gustav gathered the group and handed each a one-kroner coin from the building moneybag on his belt.

"One kroner?" asked Pieter, examining his meager pay. "Is that all?"

"Certainly not!" Gustav said. Reaching into his pocket, he produced six small rectangular badges dangling from loops of string and slipped them over each member's head like an Olympic medal.

Dagmar flipped hers around and read it. "What's this mean, 'Access all areas?'"

"It's an unlimited backstage pass," Gustav explained. "It means you'll be able to go anyplace you want before, during, and after the shows. Normal people would kill for one of these."

"Why should normal people want to go backstage?" asked Rolf. "It's just a storage area, full of spiders and stuff."

"Because they can't."

"Why not?" said Melvin.

"Because they don't have a pass."

Melvin frowned. This lesson in rock 'n' roll logic confused him. But he certainly liked the sound of being able to go anyplace he wanted. Who wouldn't?

Gustav spread his arms wide, as if throwing open the gates of heaven. "Welcome to the big leagues."

TWENTY-SIX

Skritville, Chug, Glatt, Blurpton, Trinca—the band hit a different town every night. Their act got tighter with each show. Every venue was packed, the customers were satisfied, and the money rolled in. Gustav kept things humming along. As strange as it seemed, the former slave master was turning out not to be such a bad guy now that they were all in a successful business together. The band's fame spread, and when they arrived in a new town, they were often greeted by enthusiastic members of the local chapter of the Mel-Tones Fan Club.

Every detail of the members' lives was suddenly a source of endless fascination. Birgit's favorite color was forest green. Rolf loved string beans but couldn't stand parsnips. Pieter had eleven berets, all jet black. Dagmar considered eyes and a sense of humor the two most important characteristics of a boy. No, she wasn't seeing anybody right now; she was keeping her options open.

Gustav was right about the "backstage passes," which turned out to be a hot item indeed. For some reason, people just couldn't get enough of hanging out with Melvin and the band after shows. This was fun for a while, but eventually the performers grew tired of making small talk, answering the same questions over and over, and posing for portraits with fans. (This last part presented a real problem because photography hadn't been invented yet—the band was often kept up after midnight, waiting for Gustav to complete sketches.)

Melvin, as the creator of the national craze, was the main attraction. He was amazed, and a little embarrassed, when the city council of Bubenhead unveiled a statue of him in its town square and passed a resolution declaring March 1 (his birthday) a civic holiday.

Nor did the adulation stop there. People were always giving him gifts, asking him to hold their babies, and inviting him home to dinner. He liked having friends, but this was a whole different kind of friendship. It wasn't just his company people wanted. It was usually something more—advice, hugs, and on one painful occasion, a hunk of his hair. Gustav had to increase security at the concerts, hiring the burliest men he could find—often loggers or miners—to hold back the mobs.

And yet no matter how big the crowd, Gustav never coughed up more than one kroner per band member per show. One night, they finally called him on it. Gustav reacted as if they'd insulted his mother.

"You're killin' me here! Do you guys have any idea what it costs to keep an operation like this on the road? Advertising, box-office, donkey rentals, tiki torches, security, permits—"

Even the perpetually cheerful Birgit spoke up. "I always try to see the best in people, but Gustav, I just don't think you're being fair."

"Don't become an angry mob, now. Look,

Melvin's the leader. He and I will have a little talk, man to man. I'm sure we can work it out."

"I am so glad we're having this conversation," Gustav said between bites of his shark burger later that night.

"You are?" said Melvin.

"Indeed I am. I've been giving the matter a lot of thought. What we need to concentrate on, Melvin, is raising your profile as a star."

"A star?"

"An entity. A force. A dazzling comet, blazing through the night sky. You owe it to your public. You owe it to yourself."

"I thought we came here to talk money."

"Is that all you ever think about?"

The waitress arrived and took their plates. Gustav loosened his belt and leaned back in his chair. Then he reached into his pocket and brought out what looked like two long, white carrots. He handed one to Melvin and began to chew on the other.

Melvin sniffed the stick. It smelled kind of

exotic and fumy—like tar, only sweeter. "What is this stuff?" he asked.

"Licorice root. Like candy, but for sophisticated grown-ups. Like you, killer."

Melvin gave the stick an experimental chomp. It tasted bittersweet, and had a slightly numbing, tingly effect on his tongue. It made his head spin.

"What I'm proposing," Gustav said," is that we bring you out front more. Sing a few tunes yourself. Give the audience a focal point to connect with."

"But Dagmar's the lead singer," Melvin protested.

"Yeah, but it's *you* they're paying to see. And you know why? Because you've got *charisma.*"

"I do?"

"Lemme put it this way: the name of the band isn't 'the Dag-Tones.' "

This made Melvin burst out laughing, although he wasn't quite sure why.

After the meeting, Melvin wondered just how he'd fulfill his manager's new vision. The only thing he was sure of was that the licorice stuff was pretty good. He'd have to get some more.

TWENTY-SEVEN

Melvin repeated to the band the explanation that Gustav had provided—that this was the wrong time to undertake a major financial restructuring of their business plan. In other words, no raise. They grumbled for a while but went along with it.

As Gustav suggested, Melvin practiced singing every day and improved rapidly. He began writing material for himself and started doing a song in each concert, then two, then three.

As inevitably as *re* and *mi* follow *do*, the other members decided that they wanted the same opportunity. Rolf discovered that he could sing about as well as Melvin, and somewhat louder, but the leader objected.

"I think two vocalists in the band is enough, Rolf," Melvin explained one afternoon while they were setting up for that night's show. (He now preferred the word "vocalist" to "singer." It sounded more professional.) "We don't want to clutter things up."

"'Clutter things up.' Ha. You just want to hog all the attention. You like to be out front, while I'm stuck behind the drums. You want all the glory."

"That's not true. We're all equals."

"Oh, yeah? Then how come you get a dressing room, and I had to change clothes behind a bush today?"

Melvin was spared having to answer by the arrival of three teenaged girls. "It's him," they giggled, elbowing each other in the ribs.

"Hey, babes, what's up?" he said.

"He's even cuter than his picture!" squealed the first one.

"Now we can tell everybody we met him," said the second.

"What if they don't believe us?" asked the third.

141

"Maybe he'll give us something," suggested the first.

"Will you give us your lute?" the second asked shyly.

"Sorry, girls," Melvin said, "I need my lute."

"I have an idea," the third said, thrusting a piece of paper and a lump of charcoal in his face. "Write down your name. Pleeeeeeease!"

An odd request, but certainly doable. He scrawled, "Melvin," then added, in a flash of inspiration, "luv ya." The teenyboppers went off, chattering like magpies. Melvin had just signed the world's first autograph. Feeling his bandmates' cold eyes on his back, he turned to find them looking at him with an odd mixture of envy and disdain.

"What? What'd I do?" he said.

As the tour went on, the rift between the leader and the rest of the band deepened further. Melvin spent less and less time with them and more and more with his manager. After most performances, they'd give the fans the slip and find a quiet pub where, over sticks of licorice root, Melvin would whine about the difficulties of showbiz.

"The band doesn't understand me, Gus," he moped one night. "The pressure. The demands. Trying to keep my energy level up, night after night."

"You said a mouthful, brother. It's lonely at the top. Being the only essential element. The one they're paying to see. The star."

"Gus, sometimes I think you're my only friend."

But Melvin had another friend: licorice. He'd developed a real taste for the stuff. He liked the light-headed feeling it gave him, and he thought he looked pretty cool with a slender root dangling from his mouth. Gustav actually encouraged the practice, which he felt added to his star's "persona." But before long, Melvin was practically living on licorice. The dietary imbalance was giving him hangovers. He began sleeping later and later—often until noon—and when he woke up, he was dizzy and grouchy, and his mouth tasted like bilge water.

Melvin was in that very state one morning when he heard a knock on his door at the inn where the band was staying.

"Who is it?" he mumbled.

"It's Laila!"

"Laila who?"

"What do you mean, 'Laila who?' I had a chance to get away from the loom for a few days, so I thought I'd come out and surprise you."

"Oh . . . well, come in, I guess."

She entered to find Melvin on the floor next to the bed, tangled up in sheets and blankets.

"Ohmigosh," she said, rushing to his side. "Are you all right? Were you attacked?"

"Had kind of a party with Gus last night. I'm okay. Where are my shoes?"

"Aren't you glad to see me? I walked fifteen miles to get here."

"Whassat? Sure, sure, fine. Little groggy is all. Uh oh, what time is it? I'm gonna be late." He jumped up, panicked, and started untangling himself.

"Late for what?"

"For a . . . for an appointment."

In point of fact, he was going to be late for a date. Yesterday Dagmar had—to his amazement—asked him to join her for a picnic lunch by the river to "discuss something important." This would be his big chance. And she'd be here at any moment.

"Are you feeling okay? Your eyes are all puffy; you've lost weight . . . do you have a fever?" She rushed over and put a hand on his forehead. He brushed it off and started fighting his way into a pullover.

"No, I'm fine, really. Just overslept, is all—"

Just then Gustav entered. "Morning, chief. Hey, I didn't know you had company. Hubba hubba."

"It's just Laila, Gus, from back home. Old friend of the family. She made the stage outfits, remember?"

"Hey, great to see ya," Gustav said. "I like what you did with the threads, but they're played. We need something new, something hip, something up-to-date! I was thinking of tight-fitting snake-skin pants for our frontman here. The ladies go wild for that kind of thing."

"Don't you have some tickets to scalp?" Melvin said as he ushered his big-mouthed manager out of the room. Laila sank into a chair.

" 'Friend of the family?' Is that all I am to you? Melvin, what's going on here? I thought we had an understanding. You never answered a single one of my letters. The carrier pigeons kept coming back with little signs around their necks that said 'return to sender.' Now that I think of it, that did look like your handwriting . . ."

"Yeah, well . . . I've been so busy—"

"Is it Dagmar?"

He didn't answer.

"That's it, isn't it! Are you dating her?"

"No, no, of course not," he said, focused on finding his other shoe.

At that unlucky instant, the door opened and Dagmar stepped in, wearing a short, shoulder-baring red dress and carrying a picnic basket. "What's up, Mel? Did you forget about our date?"

Time seemed to freeze while Melvin desperately searched for the magic words that would rescue him. The best he could come up with was, "Laila, I think you know Dagmar."

Laila stood up. Her eyes narrowed into angry little slits. "I know her. But I don't think I know *you* anymore."

"Hey, Lail . . .," Melvin began, but couldn't think of anything to add.

"Now if you'll excuse me, I have kind of a long walk ahead of me," Laila said and slammed the door behind her.

TWENTY-EIGHT

Melvin tried to put all thoughts of Laila out of his mind. "Understanding?" What kind of "understanding" had they had? Sure, they'd kicked around together about a hundred years ago, had some laughs. But that was kid stuff. She was just plain Laila, nothing more. Good old reliable, gray-cloth-wearing Laila.

But Dagmar was a different kind of creature altogether: glamorous, vivacious, even a little dangerous, and—unlike Laila—a fellow celebrity.

And today, he would finally tell her the way he felt. As they spread their checkered tablecloth on the grass, Melvin mentally rehearsed his words. *Dagmar . . . Dag . . . this isn't easy for me to say, but there's something I feel even more strongly about than music. Whenever you sing, my heart feels like it's about to . . . explode.* No, that was too disgusting. *Die?* Too fatalistic. *Sing?* He'd already used that word. *Break? Melt? Jump up and down?* This was tougher than he expected.

Dagmar's voice, all peaches and cream, broke the awkward silence. "I'm glad you invited me here today, Melvy, because there's something I want to ask you."

"There is?" he asked, his voice rising in an adolescent squeak.

"I want you to help me with a song I'm writing." Her long lashes fluttered downward. "A special song."

"Really? A special song. What's it . . . ah . . . about?" Suddenly he found himself perspiring. Maybe Dagmar was thinking along similar lines. Maybe she shared his feelings. Maybe she was going to save him the trouble of bringing up the touchy subject of—

"Love," she said.

Struggling to keep calm, Melvin fiddled with an apple. "Love, huh?"

She brought out her writing pad. "It's called 'I'm Afraid to Tell You.' I've been working on it for a long time. Since back when we were at the Home."

"No kidding," he said.

"And since you started writing music, you've gotten so good at it. Really developed as an artist. That's why I wanted to ask for your advice."

"Wow, thanks."

As she opened the pad and handed it to him, he wondered if she could hear his heart pounding.

"Let's see what you've got here," he said. "'Secret dreams . . . fulfilling my lifelong desire . . . as precious to you as you are to me . . .' Nice phrase." He closed the tablet and swallowed hard. "So, uh, what's the part you need help with?"

"Well," she said, taking a big bite of her halibut sandwich, "I can't seem to find a good rhyme for 'Pieter.' I mean, there's 'beater,' and 'cheater,' and 'mean mistreater,' but none of those really fits. He's actually very sweet. Hey, 'sweeter!' That's it! Melvin, you're a doll. I don't know what I would've done without you." She gave him a dry, slightly fishy kiss on the cheek, took the pad back, and began writing.

Melvin just sat there and watched her for a few seconds. Then he said, "Glad to help. Now if you'll excuse me, I have to go drown myself."

agmar never cared about you. She was just us- ing you."

"And what about Laila? She didn't even try to understand your position."

"No great loss. She's ancient history."

"So who's left? The band's barely speaking to you. And the only time your parents get in touch is when they want to borrow money."

"Face it, buddy. You don't know who your real friends are anymore."

Melvin had this conversation with himself while pacing back and forth beside the canal into which he was planning to jump. Two things stopped him: the disgustingly murky water and a sudden revelation that hit him like a bolt of lightning.

"You know what, Melvin?" he asked himself

out loud. "The only person you can really count on in this world is yourself."

"And Gustav."

"Yep. Every star needs a manager."

"You know what?" he replied to himself, "you're right."

Tonight's concert was shaping up to be the band's biggest to date. Three good-sized fishing villages—Plinkton, Plankton, and Snit—were holding a joint Midsummer's Night Fair, and the Mel-Tones were topping the bill.

"Got any licorice on you?" Melvin growled to Gustav as they surveyed the audience.

"Don't you think you've had enough, champ?"

"What are you, my mother?" Melvin fired back. "I know what I'm doing. The root. Hand it over."

Gustav yielded up a sizeable piece from the supply he always kept in his boot. "Knock yourself out, kid. I've gotta go take tickets."

Melvin gnawed on the stick until his jaws ached, but it didn't make him feel any better. He just felt woozy and unsteady, which made him more insecure, which made him even angrier.

He took his hostility out on the nearest available target: the band. "Listen, guys," he declared while tuning his lute backstage, "I'm gonna sing the opener tonight. 'Born to Be Me.'"

Dagmar was about to protest, but Birgit got there first. "Melvin, you're my best friend in the whole world, but I've gotta tell you, that is a *terrible* idea. It's not our best song, and you know as well as I do that you're not our best singer. This is a big night, and—"

"'Born to Be Me!' That's final. And you wanna know *why* it's final?" He took a few steps out onto the stage. The crowd, recognizing him from the posters that Gustav had plastered all over town, let out a deafening roar. Melvin returned to the wings.

"*That's* why it's final." He directed his next comment to Pieter. "Another thing. I'm taking all the solos tonight. These people are paying to see me, not you. I'm not gonna let 'em down."

Rolf and Dagmar exchanged a look of disgust.

"Exchange all the looks of disgust you want," Melvin continued, "but it doesn't change the fact that I'm the only important person out there. The leader. The essential element. The one they paid to see. The star." And with that he strutted onto the stage, hands clasped above his head like a prizefighter—and tripped over a stool, sprawling butt-over-elbow.

TWENTY-NINE

In case you're wondering what had been happening back in Grimstad, here's a brief update.

When Melvin and his band left on their Grand Tour, something of a void was created. But the town was hooked now, and no way was anyone going back to the bad old days. The people needed music, and they needed it *now*.

Digby was first to step up to the plate. As has been mentioned, the blacksmith was a natural-born singer, so he held auditions and formed his own group, "The Anvil Chorus." Following the age-old advice, "write what you know," he churned out driving, pounding songs about fire, water, and the raw materials of his trade: bronze, copper and tin. It wouldn't be too much of a stretch to say that the Anvil Chorus was the first heavy-metal band.

Now the floodgates were open. Inge, not to be outdone, put together an all-female outfit named "The Fishwives." They sang somewhat out-of-tune at first, but improved considerably by practicing their scales. Breadmaker Norbert recruited twelve friends, rehearsing nightly above their shop for weeks until they made their triumphant debut as "Baker's Dozen."

The revolution touched everyone, young and old. The grade school's curriculum was completely overhauled, and traditional subjects such as reading, writing, and fish-gutting were scrapped in favor of exciting new programs in vocal music, choir, and marching band.

All Grimstadians who possessed even a smidgen of musical ability suddenly found their time stretched thin. Mornings were given over to lessons, afternoons filled by composing or practicing, and evenings spent performing at any one of a half-dozen concert venues that sprang up around town.

Those who *didn't* possess the gift of music were kept hopping as well. There was the building and repairing of instruments, the promoting of concerts, the taking of tickets, the writing of reviews, and on and on. It was all incredibly time-consuming, but nobody cared. They were having the time of their lives.

The Hegoumen, however, was a different story. After Gustav whisked Melvin and the band out of town, the holy man had expected things to go back to normal. But things were, from his point of view, worse than ever. People were far too preoccupied with the new craze to make time for church services, and after three straight Sundays of zero attendance, he locked the doors and glumly climbed the steps of his tower to sulk, emerging only to shout warnings of doom.

"The parade is passing me by," he said to himself one afternoon. Glancing out his office window, he saw that a parade was, in fact, passing him by.

The Hegoumen's problem was that he possessed what is known as a "tin ear": he had absolutely no understanding of, or appreciation for, music. Even the most exquisitely rendered melody meant nothing more to him than the sound of empty buckets being thrown down the stairs.

Once, walking through town, he came upon a girl playing a comb and a piece of paper (a forerunner of what's now known as the "kazoo"). When the startled child ran off, leaving her instrument behind, the holy man picked it up and tried to recreate the melody she was humming but only succeeded in getting the comb stuck in his beard. He had to cut it out with a kitchen knife, leaving an unsightly gap that didn't fill in for weeks.

So day after day, the Hegoumen sat gloomily in his tower. And every note that came drifting up to him from the village below, every melody, every fragment of lyric, just made him more bitter and determined to regain his lost power.

The Hegoumen was one angry dude.

THIRTY

Melvin was an angry dude, too, but for very different reasons. When we left him, he was lying sprawled on a stage in front of hundreds of fans. He picked himself up, dusted himself off, and swung his lute into position. The audience, mistaking this for a novel way to start the show, cheered madly.

If Melvin had been thinking clearly, he might have seen the stool incident as a warning of what was to follow. But these days he wasn't thinking clearly. He was thinking like a complete idiot.

Success had finally, absolutely, devastatingly, gone to Melvin's head.

Donning his most truculent sneer, he launched into "Born to Be Me," a fast, hard-driving song he'd written about his new favorite subject—himself. It went like this:

> *"Got poison boilin' in my veins*
> *Big drums poundin' in my heart*
> *My eyes are gonna shoot you down*
> *Like a poison dart*
> *I'm the man that you ain't man enough*
> *   to be*
> *I was born to be me, born to be me, born*
> *   to be me!"*

The band was reluctant to join their obnoxious leader onstage but, following what Gustav called the First Rule of Entertainment ("the show must go on"), they finally shuffled out from the wings.

Truth be told, "Born To Be Me" wasn't a terrible song. It had a solid beat, and you could dance to it. The words were a bit self-indulgent, but audiences, then as now, tolerated—even expected—a certain amount of swagger from entertainers. Imagine, for example, listening to someone sing:

"I'm not particularly good at what I do
I'm average and boring and my plea-
*   sures are few*
I could tell you I'm special, but that's a
*   lot of bull*
I was born to be dull, born to be dull,
*   born to be dull."*

Who would want to hear that? Nobody.

But man oh man, Melvin was taking the whole macho thing too far. *Way* too far. As threatened, he kept choosing songs that he, not Dagmar, sang. Ever since she'd smashed his heart to pieces at the picnic that afternoon, he'd been looking for a suitable way to punish her, and this seemed like a good one. And to punish Pieter, he took all the solos.

The concert reached its climax when, during the final number, "Hornet's Nest," Melvin, acting on impulse, took off his lute, grabbed its neck with both hands, and smashed it to bits against Rolf's drum set. The crowd, by now in a dancing, shouting frenzy, went even wilder.

161

Melvin grabbed another lute (he'd taken to traveling with as many as five) and led the band through several encores. When the last song was finished, he dramatically dived headfirst into the audience, who caught him and passed him around hand-over-hand like a beach ball.

Being a star was great.

After the show, Melvin retired to his dressing room and waited for the rest of the band to drop by and congratulate their leader. He finished off his selection of locally produced cheeses, but there was no sign of Dagmar, Rolf, Pieter, or Birgit. "Maybe they're out buying me a present," he thought. "Flowers or something."

After half an hour, Melvin returned to the concert venue and found it completely empty. A few fliers reading "The Mel-Tones—One Night Only" blew across the stage. The last tiki torch sputtered and went out.

"Guys?" he called into the darkness. "Where is everybody?"

A lone figure approached. "Pieter, is that you?"

162

Melvin said. "Rolf?"

But it was only Gustav.

"Hey, chum," Melvin said. "What a show, huh? Where'd my crew go? I thought I might take everybody out for a bite. Spread a little love around."

"Nobody told you?"

"Told me what?"

"They all quit. They took their instruments and split."

Melvin was flabbergasted. "Why?" was all he could croak out.

"I think Birgit spoke for the whole group. She said there wasn't room on the stage for both the band and your ego."

"This is all your fault."

"Hey, I just suggested you should step out in front of the band a little more. I didn't know you were gonna step all over them."

They stood in silence among the gathering gloom.

"So what to do now?" asked Gustav.

"Are you thinking what I'm thinking?" said Melvin.

THIRTY-ONE

Two hours later the guys were deep into their second sack of licorice down at the local tavern. "I don't need those losers," Melvin said for the third time. "I don't need any of 'em. They can rot for all I care."

"And what are we gonna do about the rest of the shows, Mister Independence? I've got you booked solid for a month, and the contracts say Mel-*Tones*, not Mel-*Tone*."

"You were the one who said the band would follow me to the end of the earth," Melvin said.

"Yeah, well, apparently the end of the earth was a little closer than I thought."

Melvin continued to gnaw as he slid down in his chair. "Doesn't matter. I'll play solo. Be just as good. No, better."

"You don't think people who shelled out five kroners each might be the teensiest bit disappointed when you come out onstage all by your lonesome? Just you and your lute and your—pardon me for saying so—less-than-stellar voice?"

"I am an *artist*," he replied, punctuating the claim with a loud burp. "The most important person in the group, right?"

"Sure, back when you had a group."

"I'll hire some new players. They're a kroner a dozen."

"Are you kidding? With your rep?"

"Good point." Just yesterday a gossip magazine had referred to him as "Melvin the Monster."

"So how do we keep the tour going, smart guy?"

"Easy. We'll change the name, that's all. 'An Intimate Evening with Melvin.' 'Up Close and Personal with Melvin.' 'The Many Moods of Melvin.' I dunno, you're the promo guy. You figure it out."

The term he was searching for was, of course,

"Melvin Unplugged." But the concept only makes sense if there's such a thing as being "plugged," because that requires electricity, amplifiers, microphones, etc.—all of which were still eons in the future. They finally settled on "Melvin—the One and Only."

The first few gigs under the new name went okay—Melvin really put his lute through its paces—but customers who came expecting five people and got only one were somewhat disappointed. Business began to fall off.

Gustav urged Melvin to beg his old bandmates to come back, but the big shot was too prideful to admit he needed them. Instead he withdrew further and further into his new "*artiste*" persona. He would play meandering solos that seemed to drag on for days. If anyone in the audience protested, or even so much as coughed, Melvin would stop mid-song and give the offender a stinging lecture on etiquette and respect. He also started refusing to sign autographs—an easy policy to enforce, as he wasn't being asked for many these days, anyway.

Another pitfall of celebrity, Melvin soon learned, is that bad news about you travels just as fast as good news, if not faster. Word of his weird behavior spread through every chapter of the Mel-Tones Fan Club, spawning mass defections.

Now desperate to sell more tickets, Gustav dropped the price from five kroners to four, then two, then one. Since Melvin was no longer popular enough to fill the bigger halls, Gustav was forced to book smaller venues. All of this meant less money for both of them, which meant no more caviar and four-star inns. (Back then, a four-star inn was one where you didn't have to share your room with livestock.) They took to sleeping in sheds and haylofts along the way, or if they couldn't find a hayloft, under the stars. This went on for week after depressing, exhausting, discouraging week.

One rainy morning, Melvin woke up in a beanfield and faced the truth. What had started out as a first-class tour had been reduced to two guys wandering around the countryside, trying to squeeze a few kroners out of mystified farmers and shepherds. On the bright side, Melvin no longer had to pay the other band members. But it was really starting to bother him that Gustav was still keeping nine of every ten kroners they took in.

"What do I need this bozo for?" he asked himself. "I can go broke all by myself."

Melvin walked through the drizzle to where Gustav was sleeping, woke him up, and said the two words that every artist or performer, from that day to this, has secretly longed to say to his manager from time to time: "You're fired."

"Fired?" Gustav shot back. "How dare you?"

"I just dare."

"After everything I've done for you?"

"What have you done for me besides enslave me in your factory and rip me off and turn me into a licorice fiend?"

"Give me a minute. I'll think of something."

"Save it. You're fired anyway."

Gustav got to his feet and brushed some wet straw off his clothes. "You can't fire me. I quit."

"Either way. The point is, get lost."

"With pleasure. Prima donna."

"User."

"Hothead."

"Thief."

"Egomaniac."

They were both out of insults, so they turned and walked into their separate worlds.

Now Melvin was *truly* the one and only . . . or perhaps the one and lonely. He quickly learned the value of having a manager, even a crooked one. With no idea of how to book a venue or promote a concert, Melvin wasn't able to land a single gig.

He took to hanging around on street corners. He would find a well-trafficked spot, squat on the ground, and perform for whatever coins passersby tossed into his cap. Several times he was arrested for vagrancy or disturbing the peace, and once, embarrassingly, for singing out-of-tune.

The low point came when Melvin set up shop at a rural county fair, next to the cattle pens.

Right in the middle of his newest composition, a sensitive, personal ballad called "Nobody Knows My Name," a gap-toothed pig farmer wearing patched overalls approached him and said, "'Scuse me, sonny, but we're having a hog-calling contest in a few minutes. Wanna sign up? You might could walk off with the blue ribbon!"

"Thanks, anyway."

"Hey," the farmer said, squinting his eyes. "Ain't you Melvin, the celebrated singer and instrumentalist?"

"I used to be," he said.

THIRTY-TWO

All over Shivrkalt summer was reaching both its end and the peak of its beauty. Green trees exploded into blazing red, fruit ripened, robins sang, and skies were not cloudy all day.

All of this was lost on Melvin as he plodded along a country lane toward Grimstad. It was going to be a crushing blow to have to face his hometown penniless and dejected, especially after all the boasting and strutting he'd done back when he was riding high. But where else could he go? What else could he do? Without any means of income, and with winter on the way, he had no choice.

Passing fields and farms, Melvin had plenty of time to think. As a kid, he'd always assumed life would get easier as it went along, not harder. He figured as he grew up he'd get smarter and more self-assured, choose a (preferably non-fish-related) career, get married, maybe have a few kids of his own, and, later in life, take up a diverting hobby such as needlepoint or rock collecting.

But things had worked out quite differently, thanks to these cursed, troublesome, fascinating, addicting *sounds* that had ruined his life. What had seemed easy had become difficult; what had been simple was now maddeningly complicated.

He recalled a fishing trip he took with his dad years ago. Lars had hooked a fish that was so big and strong, it actually started towing their boat out to sea.

"Cut the line, Dad!" Melvin yelled. "It's gonna pull us off the edge of the world!"

"No, Mel, I can bring this fella in. I know I can!"

Lars battled for hours, not realizing that the creature on the other end of his line wasn't a prize-winning albacore or bonito, but a fully grown, fifty-ton, sixty-foot-long whale.

By the time the line finally broke, father and

son were miles out to sea. They didn't get home until the next morning, and Sonya gave her husband a well-earned scolding for acting so irresponsibly.

Melvin had been right and Lars had been wrong. How could a kid be smarter than an adult—and a professional fisherman at that? What had gotten into his dad?

Now, in the woods outside of Grimstad, Melvin was beginning to understand a phenomenon that afflicts the human race at all ages, in all places and at all times: every once in a while a person will simply decide he's right and everybody else is wrong, and nothing can change his mind. This kind of nuttiness became so widespread that the ancient Greeks, who have a word for everything, came up with a term for it: "hubris," meaning "exaggerated pride or self-confidence."

"Why me?" cried Melvin aloud to anyone who would listen—in this case, a small garden snake sunning itself on a black rock. "All I wanted to do was bring a little happiness into the world. Is that such a crime?"

The snake just stuck out its tongue and hissed. "Everybody's a critic," Melvin muttered, and resumed his long plod back to Grimstad.

THIRTY-THREE

It was just after noon on Saturday when Melvin finally dragged his aching feet down Main Street. There was a chill in the air, and a west wind was kicking up swirls of dust.

The first thing he noticed was that the town appeared totally deserted. Stores were closed, blinds pulled. The marketplace, normally teeming with commerce at this hour, was empty.

Furthermore, everything was filthy. Trash cans overflowed and gutters were clogged with dead leaves. The "Welcome to Grimstad" sign had broken loose at one end and was swinging back and forth in the gusty wind. Melvin walked three blocks before he saw the first living soul—a skinny, barefoot boy sitting in a doorway, tapping on a small clay drum.

"Hey, what's the deal around here?" Melvin asked. "Where is everybody?"

"I dunno," said the boy, who kept tapping absent-mindedly on his instrument as he spoke. "They were up late last night, dancing."

"On a Friday?"

"They have dances every night now. Hey, check out this groove."

Leaving the young percussionist in the doorway, Melvin continued along the trash-strewn street. A block ahead, he spotted the village garbageman hurrying along with a sheaf of papers under his arm.

"Otto! What's going on around here? There's junk all over the place."

"Can't talk now. I'm late for my opera rehearsal."

"You're in an opera?"

"I *wrote* an opera. It's about a hardworking garbageman named Otto, poor but proud, who finds out he's actually a prince, the sole heir to a throne and fortune in a distant land. It's jam-packed with ups and downs, twists and turns, laughter and tears! We open next week. Here's a flyer. Gotta go."

Something bizarre is going on, Melvin thought.

Passing the hair salon he saw a quartet of barbers—all badly in need of shaves and haircuts themselves—singing close harmony instead of cutting hair. At the carpentry shop next door, he discovered that Ivar had stopped making home repairs and was now crafting hand-carved violins.

Across the street, Niels the woodcutter had opened a dance studio. Melvin entered to find the burly lumberjack preparing to teach a ballet class. He explained that he had finally "found himself," and that he'd never go back to sawing logs. "What are we supposed to put in our fireplaces through the winter?" asked Melvin.

"Well," Niels answered, "I've been burning my furniture. It gives off a lot of heat, and it makes more room for the dancers to move around." Moments later Niels's students arrived. When Melvin left, the woodcutter was teaching a dozen nine-year-olds in tutus how to do an arabesque.

Walking along Main Street in a daze, Melvin saw that the walls of buildings were littered with

177

posters advertising lessons, concerts, instruments, and above all, players. A typical offering read, "Working band with cutting-edge sound seeks awesome, versatile drummer. Influences: 'Tones, Anvil. Neat appearance a must. No whiners, stoners, or losers."

It was dawning on Melvin that, thanks to his invention, Grimstad had been transformed from a pleasant town into some kind of zombie factory that turned out glassy-eyed, rhythm-crazed wackos, dancing off a cliff to a one-note samba.

THIRTY-FOUR

With mounting panic Melvin made his way to the harbor and entered his ancestral home, where he found his parents sound asleep in their bedroom. He shook his father awake by the ankle.

"Hey, whaddaya know, it's our son, the celebrity," Lars said groggily. "How was the tour? Heard you had a little scrape with your manager."

"Never mind about him. What are you doing in bed? You're usually out in the boat by now."

"Oh, that," said Sonya. "We got out of the fish business. Everybody did."

"Your mother and I worked up a lounge act. Turns out we have a knack for entertaining people. Who knew?"

"Built up a nice little following, too," she added.

"We're doing Wednesday through Sunday at the Crab House. No cover charge, but there's a two-drink minimum. Hey, want to hear our opening number? It's called 'Filet of Soul.'"

Melvin's head was spinning. He felt as if he'd entered a parallel universe. "Not right now. Listen, if nobody's doing any fishing, what do they serve at the Crab House?"

"Salt cod," Lars said. "From last season."

"And what's gonna happen when the salt cod runs out?"

"Since when did you get so serious?" Sonya said.

Lars climbed out of bed. "Sweetie, we need to get moving if we want to make our tango lesson at Niels's and still be in time for the dance tonight."

"There's a dance tonight at the town hall?" asked Melvin.

"Sure, but it's probably sold out by now."

His eyes narrowed. "Who's playing?"

"Your old band, honey," Sonya said as she squeezed into her ballet slippers. "And they're *smokin'.*"

By the time Melvin arrived at the dance hall that evening, it was clear that a major storm was on the way. The clouds marching in over the harbor were the color of a week-old bruise, and the temperature had dropped fifteen degrees in fifteen minutes. But the threat of heavy weather wasn't keeping the Grimstadians away. Men clamping hats onto their heads and women clutching at flapping capes and scarves arrived in droves.

A poster nailed to the wall showed a glamour shot of tonight's entertainment, "Pipe Dreams." If you believed the artwork, Pieter had gained considerable height, weight, and muscle since Melvin last saw him (his neck, once pencil-thin, now appeared thick enough to hold up a building), Dagmar had been transformed into a raven-haired vixen, and Rolf had become a powerful Nordic warrior.

Birgit looked about the same.

Melvin approached the entrance, where the last of the audience was filing in. But when he reached the door three huge security goons appeared, blocking it.

"Hey, how's it going?" Melvin said casually.

"Ticket, please."

"What are you talking about? It's me, Melvin, you know? Inventor of music? Cultural icon?"

"Ticket, please."

"Come on, guys, gimme a break. I'm kind of going through a rough patch lately."

"You'll have to take it up with the band's manager." Melvin turned to find Gustav practically at his elbow. Show business appeared to be treating him well. He'd put on a few pounds and wore a long, fur-lined cape, a cap with an ostrich feather in it, and a pair of expensive leather boots that laced up to his thighs. He would have fit right in at a Renaissance Faire, if the Renaissance weren't still forty-five centuries away.

"Sorry, sonny. Have to ask you to move on unless you can show a ticket."

"How much is a ticket?"

"General admission, three kroners. Students and seniors, two. Special rate for former clients who fired their manager and left him standing in the middle of a bean field, one hundred kroners."

"You're all heart," Melvin said, and moved on.

He wandered around to the back of the building. By standing on a crate he was able to look through a crack between two wooden shutters.

The band was on stage, and they rocked. With one less instrument the sound wasn't quite as full as before, but they more than made up for it with vocals. All four were singing now, and the rich harmony of their voices, Melvin had to admit, was awesome in the extreme.

"Why didn't *I* think of that?" wondered Melvin, his heart plummeting to the ground floor like an express elevator. Pieter and Dagmar were laughing and smiling and bumping hips on the bandstand.

For a long, lonely moment, he watched the crowd whooping, stomping and singing along. Then he saw something that sent his heart right into the basement. Laila—*his* Laila—was out on the dance floor, taking a spin with a hunky guy who was not only an excellent dancer, but about twenty-five percent better-looking than Melvin.

Furious now, he hopped down off the crate,

kicked it into the bushes, and marched back to the main entrance against the increasing head-wind. If he had to crash the gate, he'd crash the gate. Maybe he'd feel better once he'd given this town of ingrates a piece of his mind.

But when Melvin rounded the corner of the building, he was hit by a gust so strong that it smacked him right into the log wall. Lightning crackled on the horizon, and hailstones peppered his face. His shirt flapping, he fought his way to the front door, but it was locked. The "Pipe Dreams" poster tore loose and sailed across the street.

The air was full of flying leaves and grit. Loose shingles shot from the roof like bullets and small trees snapped off at the ground. The building's heavy timbers groaned under the strain. Melvin saw that it was actually in danger of collapsing. Jealousy or no jealousy, he had to warn these people before it was too late. Pounding on the front door was of no use. Nobody could hear him—or for that matter, the raging storm—over the din inside. He checked all the window shutters, but they were locked as well.

Onstage, meanwhile, Pieter was experiencing—as his new girlfriend, Dagmar, had so aptly put it—"the thrill of a lifetime." A steady diet of successful gigs for adoring fans had had a powerful effect on him. The once laid-back boy was at this moment confidently addressing a crowd that was screaming for more dancing and more excitement and more, more, ever more, music.

"All right, Grimstad," he yelled, "This is Pipe Dreams, comin' at ya like a hurricane. Whaddaya say we tear the roof off this place?"

And that's when the hurricane tore the roof off the place.

It was as if a giant hand had yanked the lid off a giant sardine can. All the wall torches blew out at once, plunging everyone into a terrifying darkness that yielded only to occasional blinding flashes of lightning. The bouncers rushed to unlock the front doors, but a fierce blast of wind beat them to it, ripping them open like wet cardboard. Everyone clambered over one another and poured out into the muddy street, scrambling for shelter.

The storm raged all night.

At dawn the wind and rain began to ease up. As the eastern sky lightened, the people of Grimstad, still in last night's drenched evening wear, slowly became aware of a scene of utter devastation.

Loose doors and windows were ripped completely off their hinges, leaving vulnerable the homes of people who had just been too busy making music to do any weatherproofing. Shingles that had gone unrepaired for months were torn off and scattered, leaving gaping holes in roofs. Laundry left unattended on clotheslines all summer was in shreds, draped over the broken trees like soggy toilet paper. Main Street was a river of mud. In the harbor, every fishing boat had been ravaged—either blown out to sea or dashed to pieces against the breakwater.

No one spoke. They didn't have to. They were all thinking the same thing.

"There are storms at the end of every summer," they reasoned, "but we always prepared for them. This year we didn't. Why not? Because we were too busy dancing, or singing, or taking violin lessons, or marching with the stupid marching band, or rehearsing with the idiotic chamber choir. What's the common thread here? Music. Who invented music? Melvin. Who is to blame? Melvin. Who must be punished? Melvin."

Ordinarily a person about to be run over by a runaway train of thought like this one would jump out of the way, but the fact was, Melvin was thinking the very same thoughts as he beheld the wreckage. He had experienced moments of regret about his creation, but up to now, he'd been the only one hurt by it.

Now everyone had been hurt by it.

The eerie silence was broken by the arrival of Inge, the fishwife. Her eyes were as wide as a flounder's on a slab.

"It's a miracle!" she cried, falling to her knees in the muddy street and raising her eyes to the leaden sky. "The church has been spared."

THIRTY-FIVE

The Hegoumen had spent the previous evening sitting in front of his fireplace, trying to think of a new career that matched his skill set. Unfortunately there didn't seem to be much call for a pious, charismatic public speaker with a unique wardrobe and friends in extremely high places.

When he noticed that the wind was picking up, he brought in his patio furniture and stowed his fancy hat in the closet. Then he circled the church, barring all the heavy wooden shutters. Their fit was tight and snug—with little else to do through the summer, the Hegoumen had whiled away many of his lonely hours tending to maintenance.

With his living quarters secure, he entered the church sanctuary, unoccupied ever since his flock had abandoned him *en masse* for the siren song of music. The Hegoumen had avoided the place since then—the empty room was a painful reminder of his failures—but tonight he found comfort within its sturdy walls. After bolting the doors against the storm, he lit a few torches and cheered himself up by re-reading some of his best sermons. As the winds roared outside, he stretched out on a pew and nodded off.

Now, just after dawn, the Hegoumen was awakened by insistent pounding at the church's heavy front door. He opened it and beheld a wondrous, heart-melting sight: his brother, Gustav, leading the entire congregation up the steps.

His people had all come back. They were wet, shivering, frightened and exhausted, but they had come back . . . to seek his help.

He would give it to them.

The Hegoumen flung the doors open and shepherded every lost sheep, every wayward soul, into the sanctuary. He welcomed them all with hugs and handshakes, dry towels, and a place to rest their weary bones. When all the pews were filled, he stepped up to the pulpit.

"Fellow Grimstadians. The storm is past. The sky brightens. You have been delivered to safety. To security. To me. Fear not, for you are in my hands . . . and my hands are *mighty*."

The Hegoumen scanned the faces of his parishioners. No one's attention was wandering today, that was for darn sure. He almost felt as if they were *literally* in his strong hands, waiting to be warmed, protected, shaped.

"An angry wind of retribution has blown through our community, sparing no individual but myself, no structure but mine. Those of you who have fallen prey to the sinister sounds, devilish dancing, and rapacious rhythm of . . . I shudder to say the word . . . of *music*, have been punished and chastised for your misdeeds and would do well to remember this valuable lesson.

"Yea, and verily I say, this hellish hail and these torrential torrents might well have swept the lot of ye into the sea. And given the shoddy way this community has turned its back on the gods lately, ye probably had it coming. But so deep is my compassion for my flock that I took steps to avert such a catastrophe. For in recent weeks, I have prayed ceaselessly to Thundra, Goddess of Inclement Weather, beseeching her to spare you. 'Yes,' I told Thundra, 'my people have slipped, but not fallen. They are losing their way but are not yet lost. Please be merciful. Please spare their church.' "

He could also have mentioned the time he'd put in with hammer and spikes, but this didn't seem like the time to bring that up.

Just then the front door opened a crack and Melvin slipped in, hoping to go unnoticed. He didn't.

"I see before me now," the Hegoumen intoned, pointing a bony forefinger straight at the new arrival, "the one who is responsible for the plague of indolence and sloth which has overtaken our village, and the devastation brought upon us." He raised his voice to full strength. "Melvin! Come forward . . . and be judged!"

Melvin slowly walked down the aisle to the altar and turned to face the congregation. Among them he saw his former band, whose support he'd repaid with scorn and contempt; Laila, who had watched her best friend turn into an egotistical jerk; his parents, whom he had helped transform from productive members of society into lounge singers; Gustav, whose fur-lined cape was in shreds; and a whole lot of other folks who were wishing at this moment that Melvin had never been born.

"Young man," the Hegoumen said, "you stand accused of corrupting our youth, distracting our people, and bringing destruction upon our community. How do you plead?"

There was only one thing to say, so Melvin said it: "Guilty."

THIRTY-SIX

In 3200 B.C. Shivrkalt, the traditional punishment for corrupting youth, distracting people, and bringing destruction upon a community was banishment. It was decreed that Melvin would be put in an abandoned ice fishing shack and shoved fifty yards out onto the frozen bay, where he could spend the rest of his life alone, contemplating his misdeeds. All they gave him to keep from starving was a few hooks, some line, and an auger for drilling through the ice.

"How do you like that," Melvin reflected as he trudged out to begin serving his sentence. "I ended up in the fishing business after all."

The shack was a tiny, primitive affair—rough-hewn lumber covered with bark. It was just tall enough for Melvin to stand up in and just wide enough to lie down in, if he bent his legs a little. The furniture consisted of a single three-legged stool.

From his one-room prison, he was within sight of Grimstad. He could hear the sounds of a community beginning to put itself back together—dragging rubble out of the streets, making house repairs, patching roofs, and mopping up.

An hour after dusk, Melvin saw a flicker of light from the village. When he stepped outside for a better look, he could make out people moving about on the shore, warming their hands at a cheery bonfire. His spirits picked up a bit. Maybe things weren't as bad as he thought. Apparently the town still had some firewood after all—possibly even enough to get them through the winter.

But his heart sank when he recognized, among the crackling of flames, other, more sobering sounds—the pinging of strings and the bursting of drums.

They were burning all the instruments.

He sighed a deep, shuddering sigh, went into the shack, and spread out a blanket for the night.

A little past midnight, Melvin was awakened by the crunch of approaching footsteps. He lit a candle and said, "Who goes there?"

"Who do you think goes there?" said a female voice.

"Laila?"

She poked her head in the door. "If you had said 'Dagmar,' I would have shoved you through that hole in the ice."

She stepped into the shack. It was so small they practically had to take turns breathing.

"What are you doing here?"

"I brought you a loaf of bread, an extra blanket, and some toothpaste. I'll try to get out every week or two. Just tell me what you need. I can't promise anything, but I'll do my best."

Melvin shook his head in wonder. This really was a special girl. And to think that he'd dumped her for a fickle heartbreaker with long lashes and a pretty voice. "But if you want any licorice," she continued, "forget it."

He put one palm on his heart and the other in the air. "I've learned my lesson."

They talked for an hour. Melvin told her of his roller coaster ride of fame. Actually it was more like a failed missile flight—straight up and straight down. He apologized for his nutty behavior during his days of stardom, but she took it all in stride.

"Everybody's entitled to behave like a jerk once in a while. Even you."

She gave him a little kiss on the cheek and trudged back home across the ice.

His heart sang.

THIRTY-SEVEN

The Hegoumen wasted no time in establishing a new social order in Grimstad. It was "hierarchical," which means organized from top to bottom, like a suit of playing cards. At the top of the new order was the Hegoumen (the ace). Just underneath him was Gustav (the king). At the bottom of the new social order was everybody else (deuces and threes and so on).

The local population, chastened by the recent turn of events, offered little resistance to the new set of rules that he nailed to the church door. They read as follows:

1. *No music or musical instruments. Violators will be jailed without trial.*

2. *No singing, humming, whistling, finger snapping, toe tapping, hand clapping, or head bobbing. Same punishment as #1.*
3. *No dancing. Same punishment as #1, plus confiscation of dancing shoes.*

Rule Number Three was kind of mean-spirited, when you think about it. After all, Shivrkaltians had been dancing for eons. But the Hegoumen went ahead and outlawed it just the same, partly because he feared it might lead to music-making, but mostly because he never learned how to do it himself. (He was particularly jealous of anyone who could do the Carioca.)

Freed from distractions, the people of Grimstad now were able to focus all their energy on weightier matters. This meant retooling workshops from banjo-making to boat-building, mending nets instead of nose flutes, and making jam instead of jamming.

Everyone had become very, very businesslike. You might even say life had become humdrum, except that humming and drumming were both illegal now.

The Hegoumen felt that the strict new rules were a small price to pay for keeping the scourge of music under quarantine. But all over town, another equally insidious sickness began to hamper the reconstruction effort—the entire community was coming down with a serious case of the blues.

The trouble was, music had become part of the fabric of life in Shivrkalt—not just of play, but of work. An inspiring melody can make heavy loads lighter, long days shorter, drudgery less dreadful. A catchy beat has the power to snap the grumpiest grump out of the most miserable mood.

But now, under constant threat of arrest for making—or even listening to—music, the town seemed to be losing its soul.

"Remember those dances?" one roofer asked another as they sat glumly next to piles of uninstalled shingles.

"Do I ever."

"What was your favorite?"

"That time I took second in the limbo contest."

"Yep, those were the days."

Staring into a bleak future without music, there didn't seem to be a point to building boats or painting walls or harvesting crops. There didn't seem to be a point to anything.

THIRTY-EIGHT

"This is ridiculous," Laila wailed to her parents one cold Saturday night after eating the same dinner—cabbage soup—for the ninth evening in a row. "Nothing's getting done. What's so dangerous about making a little music?"

"Don't talk like that," warned her mother. "Someone might hear you and tell the Hegoumen."

"Who cares? The entire village is in danger of starving to death. If it doesn't freeze to death first."

"I'd prefer starving," her father said from his loom in the corner. "I never did like the cold."

"But it doesn't have to be *either*, Dad! This ban makes zero sense."

"The Hegoumen says it's for our own good."

"It isn't even good for *him*," Laila said, angrily pushing away her bowl. "The Hegoumen is out of his mind."

"Hush!" said her mother. "Don't say such things."

"I *like* music," Laila continued defiantly. "Everybody does. Everybody except the Hegoumen, and he only doesn't like it because he can't make it."

"Says you," her dad countered.

Laila persisted. "But that doesn't mean he should stop *other* people from making it. The town just got a little carried away. Why does everybody here have to be so extreme, anyway?"

"Shush," said her mother.

Laila strode over to the loom, where her dad was sewing a set of flannel long underwear. "Look, most people can't make cloth. They don't even know how *we* make cloth. But that doesn't mean they should walk around naked, does it?"

"Certainly not," he sputtered.

"Well, there you go." Laila marched to the door and started bundling up in her coat and scarf.

"And exactly what do you think you're doing, young lady?" said Laila's father.

"What I should have done a long time ago." And she vanished into the night.

THIRTY-NINE

We've got to bring the Hegoumen over to our side," Laila said to Melvin in his tiny shack.

"What do you mean, *'our* side?' *I* don't even want to be on our side anymore."

"Hey, I violated curfew to come out here, and now you're gonna tell me you've started thinking like everybody else?"

"Well . . . maybe everybody else is right. I have to pay my debt to society. I can't be trusted not to harm myself or others."

"Look me in the eye and tell me you really believe that."

"I really believe it."

"You're looking at my nose."

Melvin began to pace, an activity that required

him to reverse direction every two steps. Laila turned up the pressure.

"Are you honestly telling me you're gonna close the door on music forever? Even though you know you'll regret it—not today, not tomorrow, but soon, and for the rest of your life?"

Dizzied both by Laila's words and all the one-eighties, Melvin sat down on the stool and rubbed his temples. "I don't know ... I don't know what I believe anymore ..."

"Then believe in *me*. You can trust me, Melvin." She knelt in front of him and grasped his cold hands. "I'm your friend."

They sat there for a long moment watching their breath freeze in the air. Then Melvin looked her—really looked her—in the eye.

"Okay," he said. "What do we do?"

Laila got to her feet. "I just told you. We bring the Hegoumen over to our side."

"How?"

"You told me once that making music was the best feeling in the world. Isn't there some way we can ... I don't know, *trick* him into doing it?

Once he gets a taste, maybe he'll have a change of heart."

"That's like trying to trick a musk ox into walking on its hind legs."

"It's possible. Have you ever seen my parents dance?"

"Good point."

Melvin racked his brains until they ached, but no strategy came to mind. If only the Hegoumen could experience the joy of playing a musical instrument. But Melvin was familiar with the comb-and-paper story, and if the guy couldn't even play a kazoo, he probably couldn't play anything.

"Think. There must be *some* instrument easy enough for him."

He ran down the growing list of his creations: lute, flute, xylophone, drums, horn, harp, zither, violin, banjo, tambourine, ocarina, and so on. But the trouble was, playing any of them—even badly—required *some* trace of talent, *some* shred of a musical soul, and the Hegoumen possessed not a molecule, not an atom, of either. The only instrument that could fill the bill would have to be something so simple, so foolproof, that even a total doofus could—

Melvin jumped up from the stool. "I've got it."

"What?"

"How strong are you?" he asked, putting on his jacket.

"I don't know. Not very. Why?"

"Okay, so we'll get help. People we can trust. People who aren't mad at me."

"That's gonna take a while."

"Why?"

"Because they haven't been born yet."

Melvin squeezed his eyes shut in deep thought, then opened them. "We'll get the band."

"Come on, you know how they feel about you. At the sentencing, Rolf was in favor of force-feeding you your lute."

"They're all we've got. Where are they?"

"Well, that's another problem. They're in jail."

"All of them? For what?"

"Birgit and Dagmar were caught singing in their sleep, Pieter tried to sneak through a checkpoint with his pipes in his backpack, and Rolf got busted for getting funky on a boat hull with a pair of chisels."

"Then we'll have to bust 'em out," Melvin said.

FORTY

Melvin and Laila sneaked across the ice and crept through the deserted streets of town, hugging the walls to stay out of the moonlight. They arrived at the jail undetected, but before they could whisper a single word through the cell bars, a great commotion sent them scurrying back into the shadows. Digby the blacksmith was being booked. He'd been working in his shop at night, and when a neighbor heard the suspiciously musical sound of horseshoes clanging, he did his community the favor of turning Digby in.

The burly blacksmith didn't go easy. It took Gustav, the Hegoumen, and two recently sworn-in deputies to manhandle him into the cell. After swinging the iron door shut with a clang, the authority figures went off, congratulating themselves on a job well done.

As soon as they were out of sight, Melvin and Laila tiptoed up to the barred window.

"Psst."

"Who is it?" said Rolf.

"It's Melvin."

"Get lost," said Pieter.

"I'm here to help you escape."

"If it means performing with you again, we'd rather stay in here," said Rolf.

"What'd I tell you?" said Laila.

"Okay, I deserved that," Melvin began. "I was a total jerk. I hurt the band, and I hurt the town. But now I'm a changed man."

"Yeah, right," Dagmar said.

"Look, I was in uncharted territory," he went on. "I didn't have any role models. None of us did. But I'm telling you, I've learned my lesson. In the future, things will be different. People who make it big will have our example to guide them. They'll be mature, responsible artists, not spoiled brats like me."

Somehow this prediction sounded a bit optimistic—many celebrities, would test it severely—but Melvin's heart did seem to be in the right place. The other band members looked at one another. Maybe they should give him the benefit of the doubt.

Rolf heaved a sigh. Pieter asked, "Okay, what do you want us to do?"

"Start digging."

"With what, dude?" said Pieter. "You think they give us shovels in here?"

"Maybe we can bend the bars," Laila offered.

"Hey," interrupted Digby from the floor, where he was sitting. "Give me a little credit. I made those bars. *I* can't even bend 'em, and I'm stronger than all of you kids put together."

"Why'd you have to do such a good job, man?" grumbled Pieter. "Now we'll be in here forever."

"Not necessarily," Digby said, getting to his feet. "I made the locks, too." He produced a skeleton key from his pocket and grinned from ear to ear.

Quicker than you can say "Alcatraz," all the

prisoners were free. After thanking the black-smith, Laila and the now-reunited Mel-Tones hit the road for the Shivrkalt Home for Hopelessly Eccentric Youth, where lay—Melvin hoped—their salvation. The bright yellow moon lit their way, and an unseasonably warm breeze blew from the south. As they pressed forward, he explained his plan. It would require courage, stealth, per-severance and expert timing. If it worked, they'd all be heroes. If it didn't . . . well, it had just better work.

FORTY-ONE

The next morning the Hegoumen woke from a deep sleep, feeling more refreshed than he had in years. He sat up in his bed, yawned loudly, and pounded his chest like an ape.

"Keep it down," grumbled his brother. "Do you know what time it is?"

"Whatever could be the matter, dear brother of mine? Didn't you sleep well?"

"How could I, with all the racket?"

"I have no idea what you're talking about."

"Are you kidding? There were animals up on the roof. Squirrels or something. Didn't you hear them?"

"Not a peep, fraternal unit. Perhaps some lingonberry tea will have a salutary effect on your digestion."

The Hegoumen had to pass through the sanctuary to get to the kitchen. When he reached the far side, he stopped and turned back. Something was out of the ordinary. He slowly returned to the pulpit.

A thick rope was hanging next to it.

"Now, how could I have never noticed that before?" he wondered. Looking closer, he saw that the rope was actually dangling through a small hole in the ceiling.

"How odd," the Hegoumen said aloud. Then he pulled it.

Most people think that "Big Ben" is the nickname of the clock tower of the Houses of Parliament in London, but it's not. It's the *bell* in the tower. At nine feet wide and seven and a half feet high, and weighing over 30,000 pounds, it makes a stupendous sound indeed when it chimes out the hour.

But even if Big Ben itself had been installed on top of his church, and not the humble, bronze jam pot from the Shivrkalt Home for Hopelessly

Eccentric Youth, the Hegoumen couldn't have had a more spine-tinglingly, electrifyingly, galvanizingly, mind-blowingly satisfying experience than he got out of ringing that big bell for the first time.

With goose bumps racing up his arms and down his legs, he pulled the rope again, and again and again and again. Right there on earth, the Hegoumen was in heaven. Soon his brother appeared in the doorway of the sanctuary in his nightcap, hands over his ears.

"What on earth are you up to?"

"It appears to be some kind of enchanted rope," the Hegoumen hollered over the joyful din. "It materialized here overnight, perhaps as a gift from Slipknot, God of Hemp! You want to try it?"

"Sure, why not."

The Hegoumen handed the rope over to his brother, and *he* pulled it. Gustav's reaction was nearly as enthusiastic. Making the bell clang was right up there with exploiting orphans or conning some buyer into overpaying for a doorstop.

The two brothers spent the next fifteen minutes seeing who could ring the loudest. It was a tie. Finally they fell into each other's arms, blissfully exhausted.

All over Grimstad—in fact, all up and down the coast of Shivrkalt—people were waking up to a brand-new sound: the deep, golden, gorgeous sound of the world's first church bell. Its powerful peals oozed under doors, raced around buildings, snaked up valleys, and slid out to sea. For miles in every direction, eyes opened in wonder, and ears strained to understand what they were hearing. Men, women and children poured into the streets and made their way to the source of the sound, awestruck by the waves of pure joy that rolled over them.

Everyone converged at the church just as the front door flew open and Gustav and his brother came tumbling out, giddy with laughter. The Hegoumen ripped the oppressive rules off the door and tore them into little pieces.

"Fellow Grimstadians, your liberation is at hand," he proclaimed to the throng that crowded around the church steps. "The scales have fallen from my eyes and now reside in my ears. I have seen for whom the bell tolls. It tolls for me. Henceforth, and in perpetuity, all forms of musical expression shall not be abridged!"

When this announcement failed to make the crowd explode, the Hegoumen turned to his brother, who provided a translation.

"He means you can all go back to making music."

Now the crowd exploded.

An impromptu celebration followed, with everyone bellowing the Shivrkaltian Anthem at the top of their lungs while the Hegoumen rang the bell like a man possessed. From that day on, music and churches would be as inseparable as peanut butter and jelly.

Gustav heard bells in his future as well, only his went "ka-ching"—he was already scheming to sell the new invention to churches all across the land.

"You know who should really be here for this?" he said to his brother as the jubilant party continued.

"Quite right," said the Hegoumen.

Laila volunteered to go retrieve Melvin from his tiny cell on the ice.

She sprinted down to the harbor, overjoyed that the plan had worked so well. It really was a pretty clever plan. Anybody with two arms (or even one) can ring a bell. Plus, the bell already existed, in the form of the jam pot, which Olga was only too happy to give to her young friends.

Under cover of night, Melvin and Laila and the band had rolled the heavy pot all the way back into town. It was tough going, but their task was made easier by determination, teamwork, and the fact that the path ran downhill most of the way.

The six musketeers had come huffing and puffing into town just before dawn. With the help of a ladder and some tools that they borrowed from a gardener's shed, they hoisted the pot to the church roof as quietly as possible and installed it in the Hegoumen's tower. Once it was in place, Melvin rigged up a clapper made from a hammer and a door hinge and attached it to

218

a rope, which he threaded through a hole that Pieter had drilled in the floor. All that remained was for the Hegoumen to pull on the rope. . .and who can resist the temptation to pull on a rope?

Owing to the late warm spell, Laila was sweating a little as she ran toward the bay to give her friend the good news that he was now un-banished. The few birds that hadn't flown south for the winter mistook the unseasonable heat wave for spring, and were singing to one another.

In fact, it was so warm—as Laila realized when she reached the shore—that the ice was melting, and the shelf where Melvin's shack once stood had broken loose and drifted out to sea.

In short, he was gone.

FORTY-TWO

That morning, after installing the bell in the church tower, Melvin had crept back out to his shack and fallen into a deep sleep.

He dreamed that he was taking a long voyage by sea. The trip took him to distant lands, with deserts and mountains and lakes and rivers and buildings, many of them taller than three stories.

The world in Melvin's dream was full of music. Inside a great hall, a hundred men and women dressed in black and white sat in a semicircle, playing beautiful instruments crafted from woods and metals that he'd never seen. Melodies were magically transmitted great distances like shooting stars, then recreated by futuristic-looking machinery sprouting knobs and buttons. A man with a lot of shiny black hair strummed a lute-like instrument while curling his lip and twitching as if he had a frog in his pants.

Melvin was awakened from these pleasant images by the distant ringing of the great bell. Its sound was even more glorious than he'd dared hope. He stepped outside the shack to see how the town was reacting . . . and his eyes nearly jumped out of his skull when he found that Grimstad was nowhere in sight. He was standing on a twenty-foot-wide chunk of ice, surrounded by nothing but the cold, salty, empty ocean.

I blame myself, and no other!" cried the Hegoumen when Laila told him of Melvin's apparent demise. He took off his unique hat and jumped on it in rage and grief. "Blinded by ignorance and self-interest, I never gave this young visionary the chance he deserved. Woe is me. We shall honor his spirit by ceasing all activity for seven days, praying constantly to Oblivio, the God of Unacknowledged Genius."

"If you don't mind, sir, I've got a better idea,"

suggested Lars. "How about we all finish up the boats and send out a few search parties? That way, even if we don't find my son, we'll be in a better position to catch some fish, and maybe even make it through the winter." Lars was, above all, a practical man.

"Hmm," replied the Hegoumen, stroking his beard. "There is wisdom in your words, though you are but a humble fisherman and I, a Hegoumen."

Galvanized into action by the urgency of the rescue mission, the boat builders went forward with astonishing speed, completing four hulls by that very afternoon. Melvin's parents and members of his band were among the first to put out to sea. Another six boats were finished the following morning, and soon the search covered the entire coast.

While the crews were out looking, repairs to the village continued full tilt, with their lusty songs and driving rhythms strengthening the muscle and will of every worker. Carpenters sang as they sawed and hummed as they hammered, and it was soon apparent that the roofs and doors and windows of Grimstad would be snug and secure before the first snow flew.

Well, as dandy as all of this was, it was of little use to Melvin, who kept drifting farther and farther south on an ice floe that had, after three days of direct sun, melted down to a disc eight feet in diameter. But after an unpleasant period of panic, terror, and regret, he settled into a Zen-like calm.

Life really wasn't so bad, he figured. How many other guys his age could boast of the adventures he'd had? He'd made interesting friends, done work he enjoyed, been admired by thousands of total strangers, and fallen in love either once or twice, depending on how you counted.

Plus, he'd brought something wonderful into the world—something which, even if it wasn't "essential" to humanity in the same way that food and shelter were, made life a heck of a lot more pleasant.

Thinking of food reminded Melvin that he hadn't had a bite since polishing off his last sardine yesterday morning, and he was feeling pretty light-headed. He was soon deprived of shelter as well, thanks to a gust of wind that blew his shack into the water. Now Melvin's earthly possessions were reduced to a lute, a stool, and the clothes on his back.

So he did what musicians do in times of crisis— he picked up his instrument and started playing.

Hour after hour, Melvin strummed song after song, and when he ran out of songs he made up new ones. He was still playing and singing when the last of the ice melted and he sank into the silent, chilly water. Just before it closed over his head, Melvin had one final vision, one even more astounding than the fanciful world that he'd conjured up a few nights ago. He dreamed that the dolphin he'd saved long ago was swimming toward him, smiling a toothy dolphin smile, squeaking and chirping as it came.

"What a nice dream," Melvin thought, closing his eyes.

Only it wasn't a dream. It was real.

Here's the thing: sound doesn't only travel through the air. It can travel through steel, or wood, or chocolate pudding, or even your front teeth. It can also travel through water—fast, wide, and amazingly far. The song of the humpback whale, for example, can carry for over a thousand miles.

The song of a lute being played on a tiny iceberg can't travel *that* far, but it can still travel. Melvin's music poured out in all directions. When it hit the water, most of the vibrations were reflected back into the air, but some went down into the deep, still ocean and spread out across its sandy floor. Mile after mile the song traveled, past schools of fish and through deep trenches, until it finally bumped up against the sensitive hearing apparatus of a dolphin that was practicing somersaults in a bed of coral—and not just any dolphin, but a dolphin with an excellent ear, a scar in its dorsal fin, a good memory, and a keen sense of gratitude.

Everybody has one day that, no matter how you look at it, is luckier than all the others.

This was Melvin's.

FORTY-THREE

Melvin's funeral was the best-attended in the history of Grimstad. In addition to the locals, people arrived from all over Shivrkalt. Fans, friends, former schoolmates, instrument makers, even critics, all filled the town square.

Olga brought a group of students from the Home for Hopelessly Eccentric Youth, which had been transformed into the prestigious Shivrkalt Academy for the Performing Arts and now boasted a top-notch faculty and a generous scholarship program.

Gustav steered clear of his former cleaning lady, remembering her mop.

Many of the attendees brought their harps, drums, and flutes along, well aware that the people of Grimstad had burned all their instruments and had been far too busy to make new ones.

The town square was filled with songs of all kinds.

The Hegoumen called the service to order by ringing the church bell. Then he spoke eloquently about the how the dear, departed hero had brought the village to life. The Hegoumen made special mention of the encouragement and support he'd given Melvin during his early, formative years. Gustav spoke of what a pleasure the gifted youngster had been at the Home and related humorous anecdotes of their touring days together.

Many a tear was shed. Melvin's mother went through a dozen embroidered hankies that Laila's parents had woven for the occasion. Even the perpetually detached Pieter got choked up and had to dry his eyes with his beret.

The Hegoumen concluded with a beautiful eulogy and a solemn vow to keep Melvin's memory alive by embracing music in all its forms, from the simplest bell chime to the most eloquent symphony, and to celebrate his short but brilliant life in song and dance—*within reason*, of course. (This was the Hegoumen's way of gently reminding people that a demented diet of all music, all the time, had recently come pretty close to getting everybody killed.)

Then the Mel-Tones played.

Pieter, Birgit, Dagmar, and Rolf performed several of their late friend's favorite songs. They played beautifully, because they were playing from the heart.

At first the band members were able to keep their emotions under control. But when, while singing "Thrill of a Lifetime"—the first song Dagmar and Melvin had ever performed together—she got to the line, *"it touched me in a way I've never been touched before,"* she burst into tears. It wasn't just the truth of the words that got to her, it was the way that Melvin always used to play a cool little figure on his lute when she reached that part of the song, and when she reached it this time . . .

He played it.

The band stopped. Everything stopped.

Time seemed to stop. Because right there, on

the edge of the town square, not in ghostly form but in the flesh, his trusty old lute slung in his hands, stood the guy they'd been eulogizing—hungry, thirsty, bone-tired, and dripping wet, but very much alive.

FORTY-FOUR

Ten minutes later Melvin was warm, dry, and feasting on lingonberry pancakes. The funeral, which with a little retooling had been transformed into an ecstatic welcome-home party, continued all around him.

Everything had happened at once. A moment after the crowd recognized him, Melvin collapsed, but Laila revived him with a kiss and some vigorous cheek slapping. He had to tell his story in installments, as he kept being interrupted by fans and well-wishers. His mother used up another half-dozen hankies, and Lars beamed with happy gratitude.

The Hegoumen nearly threw his back out offering up prayers of thanks to every god he could think of, even inventing a new one: Humbl, the God of

Admitting You Were Wrong. Norbert the baker ran off to create a commemorative cake shaped like a lute.

But the big news was the plan that Melvin and his now-reunited bandmates came up with on the spot: a "Rest-of-the-World Tour." Now that Grimstad was populated by so many talented individuals and groups, there was really no need for the Mel-Tones to go back to performing for the Saturday night socials. A whole new generation of players was coming up, not only here but in every other village in Shivrkalt. For music had, indeed, spread far and wide—not like a threatening virus but like a carpet of wildflowers, each different, each as welcome as the return of spring.

During their travels, Melvin and the band had heard tales of other lands beyond the mountains, even beyond the sea. Nobody knew who lived there or how they lived, but whoever they were, and whatever they looked like, they were people.

And people everywhere needed music—even if they didn't *know* they needed it.

When word of the upcoming trip got around,

the entire town pitched in. Niels the woodcutter and Ivar the carpenter immediately began construction of the biggest boat—a ship, really—that Grimstad had ever seen, and Digby the blacksmith volunteered his talents for the metalwork and rigging. Laila's parents wove sailcloth day and night, and the fishermen, farmers, and bakers donated food to sustain the band during their long trip.

Construction of the ship went on through the winter. The Mel-Tones continued to perfect their sound and expand their repertoire. In the spring, daisies and romance bloomed, and on Mayday, the Hegoumen officiated over Grimstad's first-ever triple wedding: Melvin and Laila, Pieter and Dagmar, and—much to everyone's surprise—Rolf and Birgit (who had to stand on a box for the kissing part).

Gustav got to ring the bell.

A week later the ship was finished. It was loaded up with supplies, instruments, and food, and named the *Harmony*. Lars, Sonya, and the whole town crowded the wharf for the christening. Digby cracked a jug of apple cider against the bow, and with a fanfare of horns, Melvin, his new wife, and his band began their journey.

EPILOGUE

When you think about it, there are really two different meanings for the word "journey." There's the kind where you know your destination in advance—say, Grandma's house in Elkhart, Indiana—and there's the kind where you don't. The first kind can be fun, but it's the *second* kind—the kind where you just might end up someplace truly amazing, like Iceland, Bora Bora, or even Mesopotamia—that can give you a deep thrill of anticipation that makes the hair on the back of your neck stand up. (Not that there's anything wrong with Elkhart.)

This was the second kind of journey.

By sunset the *Harmony* was already far out to sea. Melvin and Laila stood on the deck together, watching the black water slide beneath the ship's prow. The air smelled of sea, salt, and perhaps a hint of exotic spices from faraway shores. The only sounds were the rhythmic creaking of the hull, the distant cries of seabirds, and the flap-flap-flap of the sails against the mast.

"Do you hear that?" asked Melvin.

"Yeah," Laila answered with a smile. "I hear it."

ABOUT THE
AUTHORS

Claire & Monte Montgomery have been writing and making music together for about as long as they can remember. Their first novel, *Hubert Invents the Wheel*, was selected for the prestigious Texas Bluebonnet List in 2007. They live in Los Angeles, California.